HAUNTED BY THE GODS

HAUNTED BY THE GODS

FORGOTTEN GODS™ BOOK SEVEN

ST BRANTON   CM RAYMOND   LE BARBANT

LMBPN Publishing
PMB 196, 2540 South Maryland Pkwy
Las Vegas, NV 89109

First US edition, December 2018
Print ISBN: 978-1-64202-964-2

The girl with the pink ribbon had been warned not to go into the forest alone. As she ran, she could hear her mother's voice, full of loving concern, filling her ears with words of caution. Her voice spoke of darkness, of monsters, and of shadows that moved on their own. She thought those were simply old wives' tales meant to scare babies, not big kids like her.

Until now.

She could barely hear anything over the sound of the wild drum of her heartbeat in her ears and her own frantic footsteps as she crashed through the brush, but the child didn't dare slow down. She knew it was there behind her and probably gained ground with each passing second. She thought she heard it breathing.

The taste of fear was bitter on the back of her tongue. She was so focused on flight that she barely noticed the dark, gnarled branches that snatched at her face and left scratches on her arms, legs, and cheeks. One branch caught the end of her pink ribbon and almost ripped it from her hair. The girl yelped in protest. She struggled to free herself, but the ribbon went taut in her hands, hopelessly entangled.

She couldn't leave it behind. Her mother's hands had woven it into her hair after breakfast that morning. "My little princess," Mama had said.

The girl glanced over her shoulder and back down the path of tangled undergrowth. Nothing stood out, but the thing had to be there somewhere, still hunting. Her little heartbeat went into overdrive in her chest. Her every instinct told her to abandon the ribbon and run as fast and as far as her body allowed. If she escaped, she'd be hopelessly lost, but being lost was better than being caught.

The pink ribbon frayed from her desperate tugs. She set her feet in the underbrush and yanked with her whole body. The more she tried, the tighter the knot became. The air weighed heavily around her. Was it darker now too?

A sharp snap brought her attention to the now slack pink strip in her hands. For a moment, her heart sank at the sight of the damaged ribbon, but her disappointment was quickly replaced by relief. Now that the bow was broken, she was free to escape. Guilt welled in the back of her mind, but she could resolve it later.

She spun and fled deeper into the forest, where the sunlight didn't seem to reach. The trees arched over the narrow passage and their boughs twisted like long, clawed hands locked together. Out of the corner of her eye, they seemed to move—not sway with the breeze but deliberately reach toward her. Behind the mask of branches, knotted faces set with deep, dark eyes grinned maliciously.

A lump grew in the girl's throat. She pushed it down and willed herself not to cry. Already, the breath ran short in her lungs. She couldn't afford to waste it sobbing. Still, a few stubborn tears blurred her vision and almost leaked out. She lifted an arm to brush them away and didn't see the root that jutted from the soil directly in front of her foot. She barely even felt herself trip. All she knew was that suddenly, she sprawled forward and landed hard.

Pain radiated from her ankle but it was dulled by an immediate rush of panic as the girl realized she had stopped her frantic run. She rolled onto her back, and her gaze searched the dimness for a sign of her pursuer. Shadowy tree trunks rose around her, and she knew for sure they were moving now. She could see them shift position and trudge closer to where she lay prone. The movement made the ground tremble—or maybe that was simply her imagination.

The girl choked back more tears and kicked her good foot to scoot herself back along the dirt. Her ankle felt hot, and it throbbed in time with the side of her face that had struck the ground. She was smeared with dirt and leaves, and her once neat hair was now a mess of tangled curls.

Mama would be so upset. But being in trouble was better than being caught, even if it was big trouble.

That was what she thought when the hulking shadow obscured her field of view. Slowly, cold with terror, the girl whose pink ribbon had been lost to the trees turned her petrified gaze upward. The creature she beheld at that moment was almost beyond her comprehension. It had a wild and grizzled, fur-covered appearance, and its wolfish features shielded bronze eyes that gleamed in the shadows.

Patches of gray and white stood out along the muzzle. It stood on two feet like a man. That part, she didn't understand.

The shock gave her enough time to notice the fangs in its mouth. Her senses returned, and she began to scream.

CHAPTER ONE

The early winter sun shone brightly, but its warmth did nothing to thaw my numb face and hands. The frozen earth drained my body heat as I lay on my stomach in the grass at the top of our lookout knoll. Dan, our resident military expert, held a position on my right. Luis, reformed small-time gang member extraordinaire, had taken point slightly ahead of us. We peered over the edge of the rise at the scene sprawled below. A group of soldiers about ten strong had huddled all their shit around them as a protective barrier. From my vantage point, I saw a wagon, a couple of beat-up Humvees, and a horse cart minus the horse.

Their protection was nothing fancy, but these guys clearly understood that any barrier was better than none. My interest, though, focused on the boxes in the center of their makeshift hold. A fort like ours could use the large, roomy storage crates.

I glanced at Dan and he nodded.

Luis shot us a look over his shoulder. His trusty rifle

was strapped to his back, and he reached tentatively for it. His eyes waited for a signal from either one of us. The problem was that he was in front, which meant he called the shots. The three of us and the group that waited quietly at our backs currently followed him on his first mission.

"Now?" Luis mouthed. He'd given up on the subtle plea for help. As one, Dan and I both shrugged. He rolled his eyes and turned his attention to the cluster of guards around the boxes. With a small frown, he studied them for any obvious weaknesses. I clearly saw an opening at the back of their formation, and I knew Dan had noticed it too. But we kept our mouths shut. The kid had to learn. If things went bad, we could salvage it.

Luis took a deep breath and shook his head from side to side. He held his right hand up in a fist, which quickly sprouted two fingers, and finally morphed into a single forward point. "Now or never," he said out loud and lowered his head to speak into the walkie-talkie secured to his shoulder. "Go."

Down below, a swarm of friendlies emerged into the open and engaged the enemy on the front side. As I'd hoped, Luis took our contingent around to infiltrate the back while half the guards were otherwise engaged. We stuck to an army crawl for as long as possible and slithered through the frosty grass.

"Up!" Luis commanded. We sprang to our feet and hit the ground running. I drew the pistol at my hip. It felt weird and oddly wrong not to have the *Gladius Solis* right there, but I felt that to wield a god-weapon might undermine Luis's authority a little. Besides, we all knew it was overkill against presumably human opponents. Plus, I had the hilt tucked safely away on the other side of my belt, just in case.

Our bull-rush into the guards at the rear tumbled them like bowling pins. Rather than fire his gun outright, Luis used it as a bludgeon, a much quieter strategy I approved of. Maintaining stealth under these circumstances demonstrated that he had thought ahead and analyzed our best options. I flipped my pistol and head-whipped the nearest guard. He crumpled into a pile, and I moved on. Business as usual.

"Get to the crates!" Luis called. A second enemy appeared in front of me, and I struck him in the face. My concentration was on those boxes. Everything else was a subroutine and nothing I hadn't done a hundred times before.

Then I saw something new. The center crate, larger than the others, shifted. The side facing me fell open to reveal a masked figure dressed in black. In an instant, I stared down the barrel of a gun.

"Well, well," a voice said from behind the mask. The words were low and menacing. "Time's up, hero. You walked right into death."

I lowered my stance instinctively. The muscles in my core coiled and tightened to propel me the hell out of harm's way. But before I could react, the masked man pulled the trigger.

A gasp of air rushed into my lungs at the moment of impact. My only thought was, *Damn, that hurts.* I looked down as a bloom of red burst across my chest and spread so fast that it was hard to tell where it had started, except for the pain.

"Shit!" I shouted. "I'm hit!" That was not how I'd expected my day to go.

Dan swiveled toward the sound of my voice, his eyes wide. "Vic, no!" He charged toward me.

I dropped to my knees. "You're too late, Dan."

He slid beside me as I collapsed. Some of the scarlet liquid dripped onto the ground.

"No!" Dan grasped me around the torso and lifted me gently into his lap. "Stay with me, Vic. You can make it."

I coughed as my hand fumbled toward him. "Tell Luis… this is his fault." My head rolled to the side, and I exhaled a final breath.

"Vic? Vic! No." Dan laid me back onto the grass, clenched his fists and lifted them toward the sky, and screamed, "Why?" at the top of his lungs. The sound echoed through the open area. He pointed his finger at the man in the mask. "You!"

The masked man's laugh started out sinister. "Not so tough without that sword, are you?" he asked. Dan held his defiant position, and after a beat of silence, the bad guy busted out into real, genuine laughter. He pulled his mask off. "Sorry! I'm sorry. This dude cracks my ass up."

Dan's face immediately eased into the familiar gregarious grin. He stood and held a hand out to help me up. "I took drama in high school and college, and…uh, obviously, I missed my calling."

I dusted myself off and winced as my hands brushed over the scarlet paint stain on the front of my vest. "That's definitely gonna leave a mark." I wouldn't say it out loud, but the paintballs packed way more of a punch than I had expected. My left boob was not happy.

"That's my bad," Deacon said apologetically. "I didn't want to fire on you at such close range, but I was too swept up in the plot. I'm sorry."

"Don't worry about it," I said. "The point was to make it as realistic as possible so Luis can learn. Speaking of…"

I turned as the kid jogged toward me. He took one look at my chest and grinned.

"Yeah, yeah, laugh it up," I told him. "But remember, I'm a member of your squad whom you lost on this mission, and that might change things dramatically for the rest of the team."

He grew solemn. "Right. I gotta work on keeping tabs on all my guys. Or, you know, girls."

"Nice save," I answered. "That said, each operative carries the burden of responsibility to make choices that will keep themselves and their squad mates safe. You're the leader, but once you're in the thick of it, there's only so much you can do to protect your crew."

"Don't I know that," he muttered.

I continued. "What I'm saying is, I probably should have prepared individually for the possibility of a trap, even if we didn't discuss it. And I should have been more cognizant of where I was and what could have happened. If there'd been more than one baddie in those crates, I would've been more screwed than I already was." I gestured to my "bullet wound." "Assuming that's possible."

Luis nodded again. His face was completely rapt, and he hung on to my every word. I would've been the last person to appoint myself as a teacher, but he could've learned from anyone. He was a sponge for this stuff. "Gotcha, chief," he said. "Thanks."

"Hey, you're not off the hook yet." I clapped my hands to get everyone else's attention. "Let's break for a post-training debriefing in ten."

They all stopped and snapped a salute. "Sir, yes, sir!"

I gave Dan and Deacon both a look. "Which one of you is running Bootcamp behind my back?"

CHAPTER TWO

The whole company from the training exercise gathered in front of me and filled the middle of Fort Victory's second common room. We had defaulted to using the living areas for everything, including strategy meetings because no one had yet displayed any desire to enter the building that still stood unoccupied behind the garden. Aside from removing the bodies, not a single soul had set foot in that place since the general's death. There seemed to be a tacit agreement to try to maintain the fort's warm, safe atmosphere as long as we could.

To that end, the men and women before me held steaming cups of coffee and hot cocoa in their hands. We were bundled in hoodies, sweaters, and blankets against the cold, and the peaceful drone of quiet conversations permeated the room. I stood with Deacon, Dan, and Luis and surveyed the sea of faces. With a rare sense of peace, I drank in the way things were in that moment. No chaos and no intrusions of sickness or violence. Nothing more than a self-built, self-trained citizens' militia, working through its training on a normal day.

It felt awesome. We all savored it because we all knew deep down that it couldn't last for much longer. The gods were still out there. I still had a job to do.

As usual, Dan started the debriefing with a general recap. "Numbers in the casualty reports are down on both sides, which is great news," he announced. "The fewer people who give up the ghost when it's all fake, the better. It means you'll know what to do if it ever gets real. And don't forget, even if you're a baddie in training, we want you to live 'cause when the shit hits the fan, you'll be on our side." The recruits murmured. "Now, let's give our young commanding officer Luis a hand. This was his first mission in the lead, and I think he did a commendable job."

Applause rose from those assembled, punctuated by a few cheers. Luis smiled somewhat awkwardly in acknowledgment. "Thanks, guys. I'm doing my best out there."

Dan clapped him on the shoulder. "I see real improvement, my friend. Keep up the good work."

Luis glanced at me, and I echoed Dan's support with an encouraging grin. Over the last week especially, the kid had come out of his shell and had proven his worth. Hell, he was the one who'd uncovered the massive stash of paintball equipment in the first place and so made training operations possible. The least we could do was make sure he benefited.

"How are we doing supply-wise?" Deacon asked. "I think these simulations are valuable enough that they're worth scrounging for stuff if we need to. It wouldn't be impossible to find a store that carries ammo."

Dan scrutinized the inventory list he had put together after the cache was found. "If everyone has reported their usage accurately, we're still good to go for a while," he said. "I'm thinkin' by the time we start to run real low, training will be over and we'll be in the shit again."

"That works for me," Deacon replied. "How do you think we'll look by then?"

Dan winked. "Like a million bucks."

"Oh, yeah!" a recruit shouted. "We'll fuck 'em up!"

Dan snorted. "Settle down, Macho Man." He scanned his list one more time. "Yeah, it'll be fine. I don't think they used much of this stuff before the general showed up, and we all know he didn't give two shits about training."

Luis raised his hand and asked, "So who won today?" He had an expression on his face like he knew the answer, but he still asked. I was sure he'd kept a record over the last week or so.

Dan thought about it. "Well..." His gaze bounced between Deacon and me. "All right. Now, I don't want you to take this the wrong way. It's important to know that the perceived outcome of battle situations often doesn't reflect directly on individual contribution."

Luis laughed wryly. "That means our side lost."

"In the sense that we lost a key member of our battalion, yes." Dan waggled his eyebrows at me. "Here's looking at you, Vic."

I held up my hands in mock surrender. "Sorry, Luis. Deacon got the drop on me."

"No one expects the jack in the box trick," Deacon said.

"More like the jackass in the box," I muttered.

Deacon grinned. "You're merely sore that you died. It was pretty solid work if I do say so myself."

"It's cool," said Luis. "I'll take the L for now, but you best believe I'm gonna come back stronger. Next time, we burn everything we see."

"That could work," I admitted.

Deacon frowned. "Well, hold on a minute—"

"Not during training," I interrupted. "But in the field, it's not a bad idea. Last I checked, the gods are still flammable."

Shortly thereafter, the meeting was adjourned. I hung around in the front of the room while the recruits dispersed to make the most of their downtime. Dan and his men headed off to change the patrols. Deacon moved in the general direction of the mess hall. Only Luis and I were left. The kid planted himself in a chair by the window. He looked a little bummed out, so I approached carefully.

"Hey," I said. "You wanna talk?"

He raised an eyebrow. "About what?"

I shrugged. "The training? You did a great job bringing us in the back like that, you know? Dan wasn't being harsh." I pulled up another chair and sat before he could wave me off.

"Yeah, I know." Luis kept his gaze trained on the tree line. "I guess I'm…competitive, you know? I want to win, and it makes me kinda salty if I don't." He chuckled and shook his head. "That's a stupid way to think nowadays, but I can't help it. Back home, winning was how you survived. You didn't have any allies. You didn't trust nobody. If you worked together with someone, everyone else would come and kick the shit out of both of you." He tapped the side of his head. "I know I gotta adjust my thinking. It's a real frickin' process."

"It is," I agreed. "I had to do some of that, too. It's hard, and sometimes it's scary, and I'm proud of you for being all in on this. We're in a situation where we don't have a choice but to depend on each other, so we all have to learn to take care of ourselves as a group. Hell, there might come a day when we're the strongest ones around and someone else needs our help."

"I think about that a lot," Luis said. "How it feels like a free-for-all, but it's really not anymore. If I kill the group, I kill myself."

"And everyone else," I prompted gently.

"And that." He turned his gaze to me. "I guess I care. Which is hard when you come from the place I did."

I squeezed his shoulder. "You're not there anymore, Luis. You're here, and so are the rest of us. We're here for you and for each other. I doubt that will change anytime soon."

He nodded. "Thanks, Vic. Don't let me keep you."

I smirked. "You're eighteen, my man. You can tell me to get the hell out of here and leave you alone." That finally made him smile again, and that was how I left him. It had to be tough at his age and in the thick of this mess. He was too young to have already lost so much.

But he was alive, at least. That definitely counted for something.

The mood throughout the fort was drastically different than Luis's sour mood. I felt my spirits lift as I headed to the front exit. The new name over the door was only about two months old, but Fort Victory had so far held true to its title.

At first, the continued attacks had been harrowing, if not quite as dangerous. Once we'd started training extra forces, the clashes turned more and more decisively in our favor. None of the Forgotten who had shown up on our doorstep were anything like the ones I'd seen before in terms of power. Marcus identified them as mostly minor gods and their associated Apprenti, basically wandering riffraff looking for a quick conquest that would boost their notoriety.

Each force soon found out that the people of Fort Victory wouldn't go down without a fight, and with each successful battle, our collective confidence grew. Dan led small exploratory parties on raids against surrounding outposts he'd found during his efforts to map the area for training. Our territory had gradually expanded, and our supplies with it.

Eight weeks in, it was still too early to tell conclusively, but I certainly felt we flourished. Tucked into our sturdy fortress, we slowly built an oasis, one brick at a time.

That was only inside our walls, though. Outside, the gods and their minions prowled in droves. I could see them from the watchtowers at night as their eyes reflected in the searchlight beams. There was no way to tell how many lurked in the shadows, but I suspected they were like all other vermin—if you saw one, there had to be many more.

They are all in search of their own kingdoms with which to gain prestige among their ranks, Marcus said disdainfully. *Soon, this world will be overrun by Forgotten who vie to be seen.*

I frowned. "Not if I have anything to say about it." The cold air smacked my face like an open hand as I stepped across the threshold. There was no snow on the long, wildly overgrown grass, but the threat of it lingered in the atmosphere. I tried not to even consider the possibility. That was a bridge to be crossed when we came to it—if ever.

Most of the Fort Victory watchtowers were now manned around the clock by small teams handpicked from Dan's best snipers. I shielded my eyes against the sun and noticed the men on shift in the nearest tower. One of them had a pair of binoculars slung around his neck. The lenses flashed as he panned them down toward me.

I waved. He waved back and gave a distant thumbs-up. I returned the gesture and proceeded on my customary rounds outside the gates. It wasn't that I didn't trust Dan's men, but I trusted my own instincts first and foremost. And I wanted to be the first to know if anything strange appeared.

This time, there was nothing of concern. The woods were silent except for a constant whistling wind that shook the naked trees. I moved slowly so the background sounds wouldn't be drowned out by my footsteps. My nectar-enhanced senses caught nothing. I was glad for that, but as I completed my circuit and returned to the fort, I made sure to keep my guard up. A lull in activity meant nothing as far as long-term threats were concerned.

And we still didn't know shit about the situation in other regions of the country, let alone the rest of the world. I'd learned to be patient about many things, but the communication issue still drove me nuts. Especially because we had a solution already—or we would have if we knew how to make it work.

I shook the heavy winter coat off my shoulders and headed for my room. The halls to and from the residential blocks were crowded, and I didn't recognize many of the faces. Fort Victory was in the middle of a population boom of lucky survivors who'd been rescued during Dan's outside missions. It seemed like the closer we looked, the more people we found hunkered down in nooks and crannies the gods had passed over. Someone had commented that we were a colony of people who had squeaked by under the radar. An apt description, but it didn't sit right with me, and over the past few days, I realized why.

It made *us* sound like the vermin instead of *them*, which irked me because it was so untrue. We worked on creating an immovable stronghold, a bulwark against the gods' dark tide. They were the unwelcome ones. We simply fought to reclaim our rightful place.

I thought about these things a hell of a lot whenever I walked the halls and looked into the happy, earnest faces of everyone we had saved. Long ago, I resolved not to consider the past, but I had the future almost constantly on my mind. How long could we stay there? Where would we go next? Who was out in the wild wasteland right now and possibly moving toward us?

It was impossible to know, and that was why we *really* needed a functioning communications network. At that point, I would've settled for tin cans on a string—anything to make it feel that we weren't the last human holdout. I pursed my lips, shook my head, and willed the frustration down. Some things were still beyond my control, as much as I hated to admit it.

Odd, Marcus said suddenly. I thought I was hearing things until he added, *I have never seen Abraxzael willingly associate with a human other than you. There is a first time for everything, I suppose.*

"What are you talking about?" I frowned. "That dude hates humans. He still only tolerates me, and I think that's mostly because I have a sword that can cut him in half."

It would appear that his list of exceptions has expanded to include one more. Marcus directed my attention to an open doorway on my right. The room within had been repurposed into a classroom for the fort's many children. It was currently dark but not dark enough to prevent me from seeing who was in there.

"Wait, is that Jules?" I was too far away to call to her over the background din of so many other residents. As I struggled to approach, I noticed her join the foot traffic moving away from me. "Damn."

But my timing was perfect to align me with Brax at the door. He barely noted my presence.

"I thought you didn't trust any humans," I teased lightly. "Does that mean you know something about Jules that I don't?"

I'd only meant it as a joke, but his face hardened even more than usual. "None of your business," he retorted. "I have other shit to do." He pushed away and strode down the corridor at a fast clip. Others scrambled to get out of his way.

"What the fuck?" I raised an eyebrow. "Why does he have to be such a prick about it? I was kidding."

We have talked about the beef before, Marcus said. *It appears that Abraxzael may be a purveyor of bovine meats after all.*

"Yeah, of course, he is." I turned and continued toward my room. "But not with me." A feeling of general unease settled in the pit of my stomach, and I suddenly wondered how much I truly trusted Brax. One thing was absolutely for sure. If he was messing with Jules, we would have some really big problems.

"Vic!" The voice reached my ears after I rounded the last corner leading to my room. That stretch of the hallway was significantly quieter, and I turned with some unease, reluctant to get stuck in the crowd again. A few seconds later, Veronica appeared and came toward me with a huge, eager grin on her face. "Hey, I thought that was you I saw! I have some amazing news."

I smirked. "Oh, really? Tell me you found someone who can build another wing on this place."

She laughed. "Well, no, but don't worry. We still have tons of empty beds and supplies." Her smile brightened. "And believe it or not, people are super happy, Vic. They love living here. We've done a good job."

"Good. I'm glad to hear it." Positive status reports did a lot to ease my mind.

"But even that's not the great news," Veronica continued. "You know we've processed many people these past few days for intake, yeah? There's someone I want you to meet."

I folded my arms. "This is new. Should I be worried?"

"No, you should be pumped," Veronica said. She practically bounced up and down with excitement. "This lady's name is Marge, and she's an engineer."

I frowned. "Like she drives a train? I'm not really sure how that will help us—"

"No, moron," Veronica interrupted. "I think she can help us fix the radio."

CHAPTER THREE

My mouth fell open. "Oh, shit. Seriously?" A grin spread across my face. "Man, screw getting changed and taking a shower. I need to see this lady now. Choo choo! Full steam ahead."

Veronica laughed. "Dammit, she's not a train engineer. She's like an electrical engineer or something."

I frowned. "You mean she runs on electricity? Like a robot?"

She rolled her eyes and sighed. "You know what? Forget I mentioned it."

I grabbed her arm before she could turn away. "No way, Big Red. We could use a robot on our team. We've got a werewolf, a vampire, and an FBI agent, but no robot."

Veronica shot me a quizzical look. "I can't tell if you're serious or if you're fucking with me right now."

I laughed. "I'm fucking with you. That's what friends do. Whatever. I'm simply excited."

She grinned in response. "It *is* pretty exciting. Being able to find out what's going on out there? That's a game-changer." Veronica led me back through the hall. "I rushed her through as soon as I learned about her skill set. She's waiting in the front room."

I wanted to break into a run, but I forced the urge aside and kept pace with Veronica. We'd sat on the radio ever since Steph had happened upon it in the days following the fall of the general. It was sequestered in a room at the back of the fort, and of course, it was smashed to shit. I figured the general probably broke it intentionally after broadcasting his original message. That way, whoever wandered into his lair would have no way of alerting anyone else to where they were.

The broken radio was intensely irritating like he'd found a way to get the last word from beyond the grave. Deacon, Steph, Dan, and I had pored over it for hours in the beginning, but none of us had the required expertise. Marcus, obviously, was no help whatsoever. I knew that if I had a way to contact Namiko, she might be able to fix it. In order to do that, however, I needed something that could transmit.

Like a radio, for instance. The irony was not lost on me.

Eventually, duty called us all back to the responsibilities that evolved into our day-to-day routines, and the radio continued to gather dust beneath its covering. Life at Fort Victory took on its deceptive veneer of normalcy, which we accepted with no small measure of relief. But I didn't forget about the busted radio shrouded against a back wall.

Our stockpile of provisions began to overflow the pantry, and Jules and Veronica moved the excess into the radio room. Boxes and cans were now stacked around the dead device. Frank and Steph were sent on a side mission to DC to scout out any remaining government or military presence. Dispatching them in person still felt like we had given up on the easiest possible answer to our problems, but the radio remained beyond our abilities to fix. For a while, I'd wondered if there would ever be a day when it was usable.

That day might be today.

Veronica took me to a corner of the front room, where a spindly old woman with a cottony explosion of gray hair sat ensconced in a recliner. Her sneaker-clad feet dangled a good four or five inches off the floor. I did my absolute damnedest to keep my face neutral when it became apparent what kind of individual we had to deal with.

"Marge?" Veronica asked gently and touched one skinny shoulder. The woman's walnut of a face turned toward her, and two bright, fiercely intelligent eyes stared out. "This is Vic." Veronica gestured at me. "She's the one I told you about."

The old lady's eyes snapped instantly to me. She gripped the arms of the chair and pulled herself forward until the soles of her sneakers rested flat on the floor and she practically tipped off the seat. "You're the one in charge here?" Her voice was high and reedy but sharp. She meant business.

"Yes, ma'am," I said. "It's wonderful to meet you. I hear you might be able to help us with some of our tech."

"Now, don't go getting too excited just yet, kids." Marge sniffed. "I'm an engineer, not a miracle worker. If the thing is kaput, it's kaput, and I don't want to hear any groaning about it, you understand?"

Veronica hid a smile. "Yes, of course. We appreciate you

agreeing to even take a look at it." She picked up a simple wooden cane that leaned against the wall. "Would you like to do that now?"

The little old lady scrunched her wrinkled face, but she shrugged her shoulders nonchalantly. "Yes, yes. Let's see what all the fuss is about, shall we?" She hoisted herself out the chair, took the cane from Veronica, and stomped ahead of us. "I assume one of you would tell me if I was going the wrong way," she called, "but I don't think I am. This isn't my first rodeo."

"Where did she come from?" I asked Veronica quietly.

"I don't know," she replied. "But wherever it was, she's awesome."

Apparently, she comes from the rodeo, Marcus added. *Although she seems awfully small to be a horse wrangler.*

I didn't have the energy to correct him.

Marge found the radio room without much difficulty or aid from us. She pushed the door open with the end of her cane and hobbled inside. "That it?" she asked and pointed the cane at the radio cover. Her eyes gleamed and zeroed in on the trace evidence of debris still scattered around.

"That's it." I grasped a corner of the sheet and whipped it away to reveal the radio's ruined face in all its jagged, demolished glory. Marge took one look at it and cackled as she leaned on her cane.

"Is that reaction good or bad?" I asked and dropped the sheet to the side. It had been a while since I last saw how bad the radio looked, and I had to admit, the prognosis seemed grim at best.

"Too early to say." She eased in closer. Veronica brought

her a chair, and she plopped her skinny butt down on it and scooted it as near as she could to the radio casing. "We'll need a screwdriver. Phillips head, if you please."

The toolbox we'd originally brought in to tinker with the thing still sat in the corner. I rummaged through it for the proper tool and used the screwdriver to remove the front plating of the machine. The inside was a mess of dials and wires and circuitry that I couldn't begin to understand.

Marge rubbed her chin and mumbled to herself. She leaned in closer and squinted in concentration. Veronica and I stood poised and ready to catch her should she topple off the chair. A few long minutes passed. Eventually, her mumbles stopped.

"What do you think?" I ventured hesitantly. Every fiber of my being was prepared for the worst diagnosis.

This contraption utterly confounds me, Marcus declared. *There is something to be said for the written word, I think.*

"Not bad," Marge decreed. "Not bad at all." She jabbed her thumb in Veronica's direction. "This one here talked like all you had was a pile of glass and plastic." She chuckled. "It could be how it looks like to you, but to me?" She nodded serenely. "We can fix this old thing up in a jiffy. I need some new parts, mind you."

I grinned so wide my cheeks hurt. "Are you sure you can salvage it?"

Marge wrinkled her nose. "Honey, you listen to me. I worked at NASA, back in the sixties, on the telecom systems that kept Houston in touch when we got to the moon. Those turned out fine if I recall."

"Wow," I said. "Okay, that's one hell of a resume."

She shrugged like it was no big deal, but I thought I saw

a hint of pride in her eyes. "And that's only the job I can tell you about."

"What do you mean?" Veronica asked.

"I think she means she did classified work," I said. "Top secret stuff, right?"

Marge smiled enigmatically. "You didn't hear it from me."

Veronica's eyes widened, and she looked at the old woman in awe. "I bet you've got some great stories to tell."

Marge nodded. "We all do these days. Everyone here is a survivor, and one way or another, we all went through hell before we got to Fort Victory."

"That's the damn truth," I said. I scrounged up a pen and a scrap of paper. "Tell us what you need to fix the radio and we'll find a way to get it here for you." The tip of my pen hovered over the paper and practically vibrated with anticipation.

The old lady looked at me from her perch atop the chair. Her crinkled eyes sparkled with a hint of amusement. "I can't say you're not determined," she said. "Good. Now make sure you get this all down exactly as I say. If the specs are wrong, the parts won't work."

She proceeded to rattle off a list of things that dampened my new-found hope a little. We'd probably be able to gather it all at a regular hardware store, but the hard part would be to head back into civilization. Anything could be out there waiting for us.

I read the list back to Marge to make sure I had everything right. She made a few corrections and finally nodded her old head. The cloud of grey hair bounced around her temples.

"Give us a day or two," I told her. "A trip to the store isn't as simple as it used to be, but you'll have your materials, I swear."

An impish smile deepened the furrows in the engineer's face. "Oh, I don't give a hoot how long it takes." She chortled. "I'm not going anywhere. Unless I die before you get back, of course."

I blinked. "Please, uh…please try to stay alive, ma'am. We'll move as fast as we can."

Marge scooched her chair back, pushed to her feet, and gripped the top of the cane. "Well—"

Her voice was cut off by a massive, rumbling crash. The entire building trembled, and her balance wavered. Veronica rushed to steady the ancient woman while I raced to the nearest exit, which happened to be the door nearest the garden. From there, it was impossible to see anything other than a huge cloud of dust.

Shouts rang out, quick and panicked. I lunged into a sprint toward the scene of destruction, dreading whatever new surprise the world had in store for me.

CHAPTER FOUR

The pile of rubble was taller than me, and it still hadn't settled when I reached it. The dust rose like smoke and swirled in the breeze. I stood there for a moment, stunned. Only a few minutes ago, this had been a watchtower.

And people were inside it.

The thought cut through my shock and spurred me to action. I bolted toward the jagged mess of broken support beams with my sword at the ready. A couple of the guards had started to work their way out of the tower ruins, but I knew there were more.

"Stay still!" I called. "I can cut you out."

The men froze. They looked like mice trapped in a maze and stared at me with wide, apprehensive eyes. Around them, the remains of the watchtower creaked and groaned. Pieces of the structure still broke and crumbled away. I had to be careful. One wrong move would start an avalanche of debris that could crush the survivors.

I'd never used the *Gladius Solis* for this kind of precision work, but I refused to let fear stop me from saving lives. I had to work carefully to ensure these guys escaped unscathed. It was like a high-stakes game of Jenga.

With that perspective, I moved in and began to widen openings with steady care. Where I was able, I lifted rubble out of the way with my hands. The men coughed and shielded their noses and mouths.

"Be careful getting down," I told them. "This doesn't look too stable." They nodded as they scrambled through the exits I had carved.

"Help!" The scream was muffled and weak. "Help me. I'm down here."

Our heads snapped toward the source of the sound. I threw some of my previous caution to the wind and hacked away a larger portion of the wreckage. A massive support beam lay diagonally through the middle of the watchtower's former base, and as I moved closer, I saw the lower half of a human body pinned underneath.

"Help!" he shouted again, though his voice was already hoarse. "Can anyone hear me?"

"It's okay," I answered without knowing if that was the truth. "I'm here. I'll get you out."

I reached the fallen beam, brushed my hands off, and gripped it under the bottom edge. Resolute, I lifted with all my strength. The trapped guard's compatriots who had already been freed ran up behind me. They joined the effort on either side, followed by several others. We strained together to pick the damn thing up, but it wouldn't budge.

"It's caught under something," someone yelled. "We have to break it somehow."

I glanced at my sword. The blade would make short work of our task, but at what cost to the man underneath? I couldn't risk it. Instead, I readjusted my grip on the beam and pulled as hard as I could. The girder shifted slightly. On the other side, the guard made a strangled, hopeless sound.

"Shit," I muttered. "Shit!" My brain raced for a solution and came up empty. The situation seemed hopeless. If we weren't able to lift this thing up off of him, there seemed to be nothing left to do.

No. That was unacceptable. I took a deep breath and reached for my sword. As long as I was extremely careful…

Victoria, this is an exceedingly reckless course of action.

"I have no choice, Marcus," I retorted tersely. "It's either this or leave him to die, which will not happen."

You have seen the effects of the Gladius Solis on flesh, both human and monster. Indeed, you have used these effects to your advantage. I should not have to tell you it is inadvisable to expose this man to the blade for any length of time.

I ground my teeth in frustration and wondered how it was that Marcus could manage to be both right and wrong at the same time. Of course, I knew the risk I took, and of course, I hated it, but I couldn't think of another option.

Before I could formulate a reply, however, my thoughts were interrupted by a fierce female voice at my back. "*Move!*" she bellowed. The crowd around the beam scattered. In the next moment, Maya grabbed the beam beside me. "Ready, Vic? We can do this."

I nodded, suddenly filled with a renewed sense of vigor. She triggered her transformation, and we lifted together. Her hulking Were-form dwarfed us all. I heard gasps and whistles from the onlookers. More importantly, the collapsed support moved. Maya roared and surged upward until the end of the beam hovered above the ground. Instantly, the bystanders swooped in to recover the injured guard. They dragged him to safety, and I signaled her to drop her section of the load. It settled into the imprint it had left in the dirt, and we backed away.

"Thanks," I said to her as I rubbed my shoulder. The nectar gave me super-human strength, but those muscles would be sore tomorrow. "I don't think we could have pulled that off without you."

She shrank down to her human form, picked up her coat, and dragged it on. "Don't worry about it. Do you think you could grab me some clothes? I have to make sure this man gets taken care of, and I'll work better if I'm not showing my naughty bits off to the entire fort." She turned toward the place where the rescuers had laid down their injured colleague. "If he's stable enough to move, we need to get him inside and warm. There's a stretcher inside with the medical supplies."

"I know where that is," a young woman said and darted toward the fort.

Maya knelt by the guard's side. Very gently, she worked the boots off his feet. "Can you feel this?" she asked.

"Yes, ma'am," said the guard. "Thank you. Thank you so much."

"Don't thank me yet," Maya said. "Wiggle your toes for me, please." Once he did, she breathed a sigh of relief. "Good. You're not paralyzed. That's one thing we don't need to worry about."

I tore myself away from the scene to fetch the doctor

some clothes as she'd requested. The population of Fort Victory knew about Were-Maya, and they knew she protected the shit out of them, so they embraced her. Not least, I thought, because she was so damn great with people. In a group full of well-meaning assholes who were more than a little rough around the edges, I couldn't have been more grateful for her overflowing compassion.

The girl with the stretcher passed me at the front entrance, a look of absolute determination on her face. I turned for a second to watch her dash to Maya, and a swell of pride formed in my chest. The people in the fort had become a community like one big family brought together through struggle and perseverance. These were my people, and they looked out for one another.

Seeing it reminded me that humanity was worth saving from the gods' invasion. This was why I fought.

Ten minutes later, I stood guard while Maya ducked behind the watchtower to change her clothes. The stretcher and its human cargo were on its way to the fort infirmary, and everyone else had slowly begun to disperse back to their normal activities.

"Thanks for bringing these," Maya said from behind a section of the tower's base. "I didn't think about the aftermath when I sprang into action."

"You saved that man's life," I told her. "The least I could do is get you a shirt and some jeans."

"I guess that's true." She emerged and grinned as she pulled down the hem of her shirt. "Give me fifteen minutes before we debrief. I want to check on that poor guy and make sure he's really all right."

"Lead the way." I stepped back to let her move in front

of me. "I'd like to have Dan take a look at this tower and see if he can figure out why it collapsed. I didn't realize they were so rickety."

As if summoned by my words, Dan strode across the grass toward us, his face a mask of concern. "What happened out here?" he asked. "I received a distress call while I was out on patrol." Maya slipped passed him, and he glanced over my shoulder. "Oh, shit."

"Everyone's okay as far as we know," I assured him. "Maya's on top of that. But I need you to go over that thing with a fine-toothed comb until you find out why it fell. The towers are useful, but we can't station anyone up there if it means our troops are in danger."

"Agreed," he said. "I'll have a report for you as soon as I know the cause." He used his radio to call for assistance and jogged toward the tower site.

Satisfied with his response, I followed Maya toward the sickroom. I trusted her judgment, but it never hurt to see things for myself. And I also tried hard to be more visible around the fort, more approachable—which meant developing some sort of bedside manner. For that, I felt I needed all the help I could get.

CHAPTER FIVE

"Hey, Vic." Maya stepped out from behind the curtained-off section of the med room where the injured guard had been taken. "He's sleeping at the moment. If you want to talk to him, could you do it later? His body needs the rest right now."

I blinked. "Oh, yeah, sure." The realization washed over me that I was out of my element there. More than anywhere else, this was her turf.

"Thanks." She put her notepad on a table and went to the sink to wash her hands. "Never a dull moment here, is there?"

I shook my head and chuckled. "That's one way to put it. Actually, I hoped I could grab a minute with you if you have time. We haven't been able to talk one on one since we got here."

She smiled. "That'd be nice. Meet you in the common room in five? I have to file my notes before I forget."

We separated, and I took my time through the halls and absorbed the cozy rhythm of life at the fort. Kids put puzzles together under the watchful eyes of their parents. An older man wearing a bandana on his head gave me a grin and a wave as he methodically mopped the hallway floor. In the common room itself, two teens stood on stepladders and cleaned the windows. I could even smell the aroma of food wafting in from the mess hall.

The gods were still out there, but humanity wasn't finished yet. We were really making a go of it.

Maya showed up not too long after I made myself comfortable on one of the sofas. She took a seat on the cushion beside me. "Man, it feels good to sit," she said and closed her eyes. "I feel like I'm constantly on the run."

"You kind of are," I said with a smirk. "People probably think you never sleep."

"I've found that naps are a godsend," she said. "Catnaps."

"Dog naps," I responded.

She rolled her eyes but smiled. "If anything, they'd be *wolf* naps. But I grab them when I can and pray the cumulative sleep deficit doesn't catch up with me during a crisis." She paused. "Although I will say, there haven't been a lot of real disasters since we took the place over. This might be the first one." She looked proud. Tired, but proud.

"It's incredible that we haven't lost anyone," I said. "And it's all thanks to our amazing chief medical officer."

Maya smiled. "Well, I do my best, and conditions here are certainly much better than they were in the woods. Plus, no one has been murdered, which is great. But we're still a far cry from pre-apocalypse standards. Our medicine stock is limited, and I mean, I'm a vet. I didn't go to med school, so I can't definitively give diagnoses if something major goes wrong." She frowned. "Don't get me wrong. I'm really, really glad we're here. But it feels like we're sitting on a time bomb."

I'd had that feeling myself more than once. Hearing it articulated by Maya only strengthened my determination to get the ball rolling as far as the gods were concerned.

"I know what you mean," I said. "The good news is, we'll finally make some headway on the communications front. Veronica found someone who can fix the radio."

Her expression brightened. "Hey, that's great! I'm dying to know what the situation looks like beyond our little sphere. How many people out there haven't been as fortunate as our little community?"

I sighed. "I know. Honestly, I'm a little afraid to find out, but I have to know the circumstances. And at the same time, I think I'm the only one with a weapon like this, so things can't look too good everywhere that I'm *not*." I glanced at her. "I'm not in a lot of places."

Maya placed her hand on my arm. "You're doing great, Vic. We're so thankful for everything you've done. The bottom line is that none of us would be here if not for you." She chewed her lip. "That said…"

"You won't offend me, Maya," I replied. "Trust me. I want what's best for the group, and if you know what that might be, I'm all ears. At this point, there are no stupid suggestions."

"Yeah. But we worked so hard to get here that it seems like…" She trailed off. "I guess things are always changing, and the longer we stay here, the more I can't help thinking that this isn't a tenable long-term solution."

I frowned. "Why not?"

She shrugged. "We can maintain our defenses and make

regular supply runs, but even though this setup is sustainable, we still live in what basically amounts to a prison for however long this lasts." She looked at me. "I don't want that for you, or myself, or any of these people. It's good that we're safe, but we can't stay locked up in here forever."

I nodded slowly as I considered how I wanted to answer. Her point struck a deeper chord with me than I wanted to admit. Part of what had made life bearable in the hellish underbelly of New York City was the complete and utter freedom from everything, even laws. I hadn't answered to anyone or anything, except the gnawing desire for justice against my parents' killer, and that had been thrilling in a lot of ways. Granted, I was no longer the unprincipled wild child I'd been back when my quest against Rocco Durant first began, but the idea of spending the rest of my days confined in the fort for safety's sake hardly appealed to me.

The world did not belong to the gods. It belonged to us. And I needed to get off my ass and take it back.

"We have a ton of work to do still," I said to Maya. "But I promise, there's an end to this. I'm not sure when, and I'm not sure how it'll happen yet. All that matters is that we'll go after the jackasses who think they can take over. We won't hide here. We're merely regrouping, training new people, and building our strength. The gods caught us with our pants down when they invaded. I won't let that happen again."

"That sounds good to me," she responded. "I simply wanted to know we're not dead in the water, is all." She gestured around the room. "Two months ago, this felt like paradise to me. I pushed hard for it. Now, I know it's a necessary compromise. I hope we don't have to make it forever."

I shook my head vehemently. "We won't. I won't let you down, Maya. You or anyone else in Fort Victory."

"Of course you won't, Vic." She smiled. "You never have."

We walked out of the common room together and she peeled off to return to the infirmary. I was on my way to take that long-deferred shower when I heard purposeful bootsteps behind me. I turned to see Dan, fresh from outside and his cheeks ruddy with the cold. "I have a preliminary report," he said, slightly out of breath.

"That was fast," I said.

He shrugged. "It wasn't hard to reach a conclusion once we found what we were looking for."

The phrasing piqued my interest. "And what was that?"

Dan held his hand out and opened his fingers. A few thick bolts rested in his upturned palm. "It was a little hard to determine at first, but once we recovered and organized the supports, we saw a pattern. That tower was riddled with loose bolts. It was simply waiting to come down."

I furrowed my brow. "What the hell does that mean?"

"That's the million-dollar question." He stuck the bolts in his pocket. "My guess is that the general did it when he moved in, perhaps to keep his guys on their toes or to thwart any attempt at a coup. Or this place is simply in worse shape than it looks. Either way, I've dispatched task forces to the other towers to make sure they're sound. I'll let you know what we find."

"It's been months," I said. "Why did it take so long to fall?"

Again, he shrugged. "Not all of them were compromised but enough to throw structural integrity off. It's possible the general didn't even know and we drew the short straw. In any case, we can make sure it never happens again."

"Right. Good. Go do that."

He left and I went to my room, gathered a towel and some fresh clothes, and sat on the edge of the bed for a few minutes as I mulled things over. Maybe that crazy old coot had meant for us all to be part of his grand sacrifice—including his own men. "Hey, Marcus? Sorry I snapped at you before. I was stressed out."

It has all worked out for the best, Victoria. What troubles you? You never apologize unless your mind is heavy.

"Wow, that's cold," I said. "But also true." I ran my fingers through my hair. "I want to be prepared for what lies ahead, and I realize now that it's already pretty bad, isn't it? These fuckers are totally ruthless."

I believe it would be best for you to focus on one thing at a time, rather than get mired in possibilities. There is nothing you have learned here about the Forgotten that you did not already know.

"Yeah." I sucked in a deep breath and told my mind to be quiet. There was no point in getting nervous about a bridge we hadn't crossed yet. "Okay. What's next, then?" That last question was more to me than to Marcus, but he answered anyway.

The future device requires repair.

"It's not a future device, dude." I laughed a little. "Radios have been around for over a hundred years."

And I have been around for two millennia. Almost all things are the future to me.

"Nah," I said, still smiling. "You're the distant past. When this is over, we'll find you a nice museum to settle down in."

He grumbled. *I find this retirement plan...objectionable.*

CHAPTER SIX

I handpicked the squad for the radio run—it was me, Deacon, Dan, Luis, and a couple of Dan's best guys. Dan nailed down the location of a place that might have the parts we needed. "Twenty miles out," he said. "It's a medium-sized town, so that might mean it's more dangerous, but it has a hardware store. And a mall, if that fails. I think it's extremely likely that we'll run into someone down there, so it's best to be prepared for anything."

"By 'anything' you mean 'the worst,' right?" I joked.

He winked. "You got it. But I, for one, will expect the best."

"We don't have any intel at all about possible enemies?" Deacon asked. "Not that I don't think we can deal with whatever we find, but it'd be nice to know in advance."

Dan pointed at my sword. "Unless that thing is secretly a metal detector for all things unholy, we're shit out of luck." They looked at me expectantly.

I made a face. "What, like it'll start to screech every time a god is near? I don't think so." I patted the hilt on my hip. "Don't worry about it. We can handle this. We're cool."

Deacon smirked. "Some of us are, anyway." He gave Dan a meaningful look. They high-fived.

"I take it back," I said. "I'm cool. You guys are lame."

We loaded into the trucks and headed onto the road. Deacon and I led the way in the vehicle with the smaller cab, armed with a map Dan had drawn us from his satellite information. The highway was long and emptier than ever. Cars stood abandoned on the pavement although all their headlights were now dead. I hoped their occupants had fared better.

Deacon glanced in the mirrors as we drove. "I don't think I'll ever get used to a sight like this," he said.

"Good," I answered. "We'll put it all back to normal, so you don't have to."

"I look forward to that day." We reached an open stretch, and he put his foot down on the gas pedal. The engine rumbled. "One good thing about the dissolution of the police force is that we're allowed to have a little fun."

"Weren't you a cop at some point?" I asked.

"It seems like another lifetime now." Deacon kept his eyes on the road. "To answer your question, yes. But doing the work doesn't mean I always believed in it, or that I can't appreciate the joy of driving real damn fast on a clear road." Having said that, he stepped on the brake almost guiltily. "But I better make sure we don't lose the others."

"Uh huh." I nudged him playfully. "Show off."

Deacon laughed. "Caught me. Any chance to look good in front of the resident badass." Our eyes met in the mirror.

I smirked. "Talk is only gonna get you so far, Agent St.

Clare." I held his gaze for a few moments longer before the smirk turned into a laugh. "It'll have to be later, though. We have to take care of business first."

"You know what they say about all work and no play," he quipped. But I could see him getting into the zone as we drew closer to our destination. The telltale signs of urban sprawl popped up along the edges of the highway. Restaurant and hotel signs dotted the landscape that rolled by outside the window.

Deacon glanced at the map and pulled off on a long, curving exit ramp that brought us down onto the main road of a sizable town. It had undoubtedly once been lively and bustling, like so many of the places we passed. As it stood now, the sheer emptiness was overwhelming.

"Keep an eye out for a hardware store," I said. "Or that mall Dan mentioned."

"Let's do the hardware store first. I have a feeling we might regret the mall." He cruised down the center of the street and paid little mind to the streetlights still hanging overhead.

"In case of more zombies?" I asked.

"More *anything*, really."

We lapsed into silence for the next few minutes, and each of us diligently surveyed the surroundings.

I tapped his arm when I saw a weathered yellow sign on a pole. "Look, there's a Value Hardware."

"Bingo," Deacon said. He stuck on his blinker and steered into the lot.

"I like how you blatantly disregard stuff like lanes and traffic lights but remember your blinker," I teased as I opened my door.

"Some things are non-negotiable," he responded.

We joined Dan, Luis and our two support guys on the asphalt. The six of us studied the front windows of the store.

"What's the plan?" Dan asked. "Grab and go?"

I fished in my pocket for Marge's list and passed it around the huddle. "Here's what we need. Memorize as much as you can and grab whatever you see when you get in there. If we've got extras, that's great. It means we won't be completely screwed if the thing breaks again." I hesitated. "And if you see something unfriendly, holler. We'll back you up." I surveyed my team. "Any questions?"

Dan shook his head. "It sounds simple enough. Let's get this done."

The automatic doors still worked in the front of the store. As on all the supply runs before, we stepped into an eerie oasis of stillness, a snapshot of a store suspended in time. There were more signs of distress there than in other places—merchandise on the floor, an abandoned employee vest with the nametag still attached splayed out on the tile, and a pricing gun that lay on its side where someone had evidently dropped it in a panic. But there was no blood, only signs of general chaos.

I clapped my hands. The sound rang out like a gunshot through the store. Dan's two men jumped and wheeled to look at me.

"Sorry," I said with a smile. "It's time to make like this is a game show and haul some serious ass. No one's here right now, but they could easily show up, and I'd rather not be caught in the middle of our shopping spree."

"You heard the lady," Dan said. "Scramble!"

I grabbed a basket off the rack near the front and darted down the aisles in search of anything that even looked like what we needed. Whole rolls of wiring went into the basket, as did tools and circuit boards and packets of tiny screws.

"Get the brand names!" I yelled to the others. "We're not paying for shit, so you might as well."

They laughed.

I felt pretty good. Oddly, these little errands were some of the times when I felt most at ease. They were fast-paced, I knew exactly what I needed, and I was always on the edge of a full-on adrenaline rush, ready for a fight.

This time, it didn't look like we'd have to worry about any trouble. In the empty checkout lanes, we swiped some bags for our stuff, double-checked the list, and headed out with our arms full.

"I'd call that a roaring success, Dan proclaimed triumphantly. The words had barely left his mouth when they were abruptly punctuated by the crash of shattering glass. "What the hell was that?"

Luis's mouth dropped open. "Over there." He pointed. "Revenge of the Bros!"

At first, I had no idea what he was talking about. Then I followed the direction of his finger and saw a whole brigade of all too familiar bronzed beach bodies pour out of the broken front window of the fitness center next door.

"Are you kidding me?" I clutched my bag tighter. "I thought we left these meatheads in the city."

"They didn't die?" Deacon asked, bewildered. "Or, I don't know, turn back into normal people?"

"After that much tanner?" I asked. "There's no hope."

"Point taken."

The bodybuilders in front put their heads down like bulls and charged headlong in our direction. Nothing appeared to deter them in any way—they raced over curbs, uneven grass, and the concrete bars demarcating the ends of the parking spots.

Deacon dropped his bag and drew his gun. "Fight!" he shouted.

They may be weaker without Beleza around to bolster them, Marcus advised. *However, if they were converted of their own free will, his absence will not matter much at all. They may simply remain under his thrall as well. I am not sure of the length of his reach or his current location.*

"He might be close," I muttered. "Noted."

The good thing about Beleza was that he wouldn't be hard to spot if he *did* show his gleaming face. The guy would've stuck out anywhere, but I didn't have time to think about that, even if I wanted to. His minions had covered the ground between us in a shockingly small space of time.

I had barely enough time to draw my sword before it was buried in the manscaped chest of a beach volleyball enthusiast gone wrong. His piercing blue eyes went wide and stayed that way. His features hardened, as did his hands around the sword's hilt. I pried the weapon free, and his fingers broke off. There was no blood or even bones in the wounds. He was bronze, through and through.

"I saw these guys in New York," Luis said. His rifle rattled off an automatic burst, and I saw another bronzed man become a statue. "What the fuck are they doing here?"

"Who knows?" Another took a powerful swing at me

and I lopped his right arm off by reflex. Unbalanced, he lurched forward and received a sword in the stomach. "Get rid of them and let me know if you see anything bigger."

Luis shot again. "I better not."

I still had my eyes peeled for Beleza himself, even though I was fairly sure he would've made himself known if he was there. These dudes were mostly scantily clad sluggers and no match for the sword. I decorated the parking lot with weird, grotesquely hyper-realistic statues of beefy men in thongs.

"It looks like an art installation," Deacon commented. "Do you think we could get a grant?"

"The National Endowment's never seen anything like it," I replied.

"Uh oh." Dan stared at the broken window of the gym. "I retract what I said about a roaring success."

Two musclebound humanoids, even bigger and bulkier than the rest, emerged from the fitness center and wielded long heavily weighted bars. Their faces were glued in permanent weightlifters' grimaces, and the veins on their arms and necks protruded. They spun the weights like staffs, so fast that I could hear them slice through the air.

"You jinxed it, Dan," I said. "Hang back. I'll cut those things down to size." The sword hummed in my hand.

Aim carefully, Marcus said. *They will likely attempt to crush your skull.*

"They can have it," I said lightly. "It's pretty empty anyway."

The nearest guy lifted his weapon above his head. I dashed in and swept my blade up from the underside. A few sparks flew as the metal made contact before the two pieces of the bar flew apart. I gutted the wielder before he even had the chance to figure out his next move.

His partner, on the other hand, proved to be a little savvier. He had deflected half the flying weight, and now he brought his staff down toward my head. I flung my sword arm up and felt the *Gladius Solis* cleave through something. The edge of a bundle of weights clipped my ribs as it fell and a dull pain crashed through my side. I teetered, regained my footing, and parried the second strike. The cut end of the weight bar glowed and smoked, inches from my skin. Beleza's minion reared back. I took the opportunity to run him through cleanly in more or less the spot where his weight had hit me.

"That's payback for the bruise I'm gonna have tomorrow," I said.

Deacon gave me a look. "Now who's showing off?"

"Oh, please." I waved him off. "If I was showing off, I wouldn't have gotten hit."

"To be fair," he said, "that was more about physics than anything else."

"It doesn't matter." I walked toward the trucks. "My perfect record is ruined." I stopped dead in my tracks. "Wait a minute. Where the fuck are the bags?" Our sweet haul from the hardware store was nowhere to be seen. "Oh, no. No, no, no." I grabbed my head in both hands and squeezed. "They didn't get anywhere near the damn trucks. We made sure of it."

"The bags?" Deacon's look of confusion morphed into one of equal horror. "Shit."

"How the fuck did this happen? What do they even need with all that stuff?" Legitimate nausea crept into the back of my throat. I looked toward the store. "We cleaned that place out—"

"Looking for this?"

I turned so fast I practically gave myself whiplash, only to see Luis sitting in the bed of one of the trucks with a huge, shit-eating grin on his face. He had every bag in there with him, laid down on its side so I wouldn't see it. "You little—" I ran over and flicked his ear before he could dodge. The pain didn't stop him from cracking up.

"You shoulda seen your face just now," he hooted. "That was straight-up gold." Out of the corner of my eye, I could see Deacon, Dan, and the two other guys struggle to keep their poker faces. Truth be told, so did I. Luis was a funny kid.

Even if it was at my expense.

"I'm glad you jerks think so," I said and stalked to the driver's side of my truck. "I'm driving back. Good job on this run or whatever." But before I shut the door, I shot them all a massive, goofy grin. "Last one back to the fort's a statue in a man-thong."

CHAPTER SEVEN

Fifteen miles of breakneck highway racing later, the lighthearted mood was on the backburner again in my and Deacon's cab. For the last five miles of the journey, I fretted quietly about whether or not the radio could actually be fixed or if Marge was merely quirky and bluffing. Everything she'd said about her past experiences was unsubstantiated, and yet, I'd trusted her. My excitement over the prospect of a fixed radio trumped all the lessons I had learned about blind faith.

I felt more nervous than doubtful, though. I was so desperate to hear something—*anything*—about the outside world that I didn't want to even consider the idea that the radio might be unfixable. Still, it had looked smashed beyond repair to me.

We pulled into our spot outside Fort Victory, and I couldn't shake the mounting apprehension as I killed the engine. I didn't say much, simply grabbed some bags and rounded up everyone else. Dan and Luis still laughed and joked with one another, but by the time we made it to the radio room, I was ready to jump out of my skin.

"Luis," I said. "Do you know anything about radios?"

"Me?" He laughed. "I told you the first time we looked at this mess, I learned how to put computers and electronics and stuff like that together when I was younger. I never said I knew how to bring them back from the dead."

"If someone else did the heavy lifting, could you help?" I sorted through the contents of the bags at light-speed and put it all into piles that I hoped Marge would be able to navigate easily.

"I can do some of the heavy lifting," Luis said quickly. "I remember enough, I think." He frowned. "What are you doing?"

"I'm streamlining the process as much as I can," I answered. "And when I bring her in, you're gonna be her new best friend until that radio is functional again."

"Her?" Luis arched his eyebrows.

Dan moved in and took the list. "We'll handle the prep. You go get her."

"Who's 'her?'" Luis asked.

"You'll find out," Dan said.

I located Marge in the same place I'd met her, perched in a chair in the front room. Her dark eyes scanned her surroundings like laser pointers. I almost heard the beeping of a target system when they locked onto me.

"Hello, dear," she said as I made my way to her. That high, thin voice cut through the room and straight to my ears. "I trust you're doing well on my little scavenger hunt?"

The words "scavenger hunt" did little to inspire confidence in me, but I hid my feelings behind a falsely enthusiastic expression. "Actually, we just finished it."

"Oh!" Her crinkly eyes lit up with a mischievous sparkle. "I must say, I'm impressed."

I shrugged modestly. "I guess you could say I was dedicated to the challenge." Carefully, I offered the tiny old woman my arm. "We've put the supplies in the radio room if you'd like to take a look."

"Whatever you say, dear." Marge took one of my hands in both of hers and hopped down off the chair. Her cane was hooked over one of the arms, and I handed it to her.

"I'll have assistants, won't I?" she asked and gestured vaguely at her face. "These old eyes and hands aren't what they used to be."

"You sure will," I said. "I assembled a team for you."

"You're too kind." Once we reached the hall, she released my hand and went ahead. She moved so fast that I didn't have time to warn anyone in the radio room about her arrival. The door was open, and she walked right in.

I heard Luis say, "Are you lost, ma'am? Let me help you."

"You must be my assistant," Marge said. "In which case, you can absolutely help me. This job is too big for one old woman to handle alone, you know?"

That was when I rounded the corner into the doorway. Luis stared at me, dumbfounded. He motioned toward Marge's back and mouthed, "Her?"

I nodded and grinned. "I see you've already introduced yourself to Luis, here. Consider him at your beck and call for the duration of the project. Anything you need or want, he's your man." I could see his intense desire to object but bless his heart, he kept his mouth shut. He knew we needed her as much as I did.

If I'd been paying him, I would've given the kid a raise.

Dan was still there too, and as the great restoration got underway, he brought in more helping hands. Even with three personal assistants, the work was slow and painstaking, and Marge was clearly not the easiest boss to work under. After the first hour, her voice was like listening to nails on a chalkboard.

It was a good thing I couldn't sit still anyway. I wanted to be in there and bear witness to the process, but I constantly jumped up and paced circuits of the room, which wasn't that big to begin with. Also, I had a nearly pathological need to monitor the radio's progress, and that annoyed everyone who actually worked on it. It didn't take long for Luis and Dan to put their tools down, look me dead in the eye, and say, "Vic, you have to leave."

"You're driving us nuts," Luis added helpfully. "You keep walking in circles like that, you're gonna make me seasick."

"And this is a landlocked state," said Dan.

Marge interjected, "No distracting the personnel."

I huffed. "Fine. See you guys later. Let me know when it's done." I slipped out of the room and resumed my pacing up and down the hallway outside. It *was* better, I had to admit. More space and less irritated glares. I walked up and down that corridor until my legs were too exhausted for me to continue and I sat with my back to the wall. Hours passed in fitful dozing while I listened intently for any sign of progress on the other side of the door. Occasionally, someone would leave to get a snack or go to the bathroom, but no one gave me a meaningful update.

They probably thought I would eventually go away. Instead, when I decided I couldn't sit and catnap anymore, I stood and resumed my pacing. The back hallway was not near a window, so I had no idea what time it was. I fiddled absently with Marcus's medallion while I moved. He had been quiet throughout this whole process. Even he didn't want to deal with me in this state.

"Vic?" I was so lost in my own little world that the first utterance of my name didn't register. "Vic? Are you okay?"

Jules stood in front of me, a worried look on her face. "Oh, hey, Jules. I've been exiled from the radio room, that's all."

"What's wrong?" she asked. "It's not going well?"

"I think it's going fine," I said. "I *hope* it's going fine. I'm anxious about it, and that makes everybody crazy. They have enough to do without me hovering."

"Well, that's true." She took me by the arm and led me to the nearest chair. "Sit down for a minute. You're making me jumpy just looking at you."

I didn't want to sit down, but I did as I was told. All the energy that had been expressed through pacing immediately bubbled up in my core. I fidgeted. "I just…I want it to be over. I want to know if it'll work."

"It will," Jules said. She put her hands on my shoulders. "Try to relax, okay? Working yourself up won't make them go any faster or the wait any easier. You saw what shape that radio was in. It'll take time."

"Yeah." I had already given myself the beginnings of a headache. "I don't have any patience right now, and that's a problem."

"Let's try this," she suggested. "Is there something else

you can think about instead? Sometimes, a distraction is the best medicine. Look at me and think of anything else. We'll talk about it if you want. I'll get you some coffee."

She went toward a coffee machine situated on one of the tables in the closest common room. I stayed on my chair, watched her select a mug, put a filter in the machine, and fill up the grounds. She pressed the button, and as she watched it brew, a weird memory surfaced in my mind. Jules and Brax had stood alone in that converted classroom, talking. About what? Those two were like night and day.

This was my chance to get to the bottom of it.

She came back with the cup in her hands and transferred it to me. "Careful, it's hot." She'd stuck a stirrer in the liquid, although traces cream and sugar on top indicated I should stir it.

"Thanks," I said. "I decided what I want to talk about."

"Oh yeah?" She beamed. "See? I knew you could do it."

"What were you and Brax discussing in that room?" The bluntness was calculated to catch her off guard, to make her slip and show her hand. I knew Jules better than I'd known myself for a long time. Public defender or not, if she thought she could keep a secret from me, she was sorely mistaken.

"What?" The shock manifested clearly on her face for a split second before she managed to mask it.

"I saw you," I pressed. "You left before I could get in there and ask you what was up."

Jules hesitated and pressed her lips together. "That's private," she said at long last.

Her response shocked me. "What? Jules, I can count on

one hand the number of times you've said that to me in your life. And now you're having private conversations with a demon?" I paused for emphasis. "You know that's what he is, right?"

"I know that." Her exasperated tone of voice suggested that she had expected this type of reaction. "He told me himself. He's been very forthright." She folded her arms. "You've spoken with him more than I have. You should know."

"I don't speak to him in private anywhere, let alone in dimly lit side rooms," I insisted. "What's going on here, Jules? Whatever it is, you don't have to hide it from me."

She gave me a skeptical once-over. "You're literally judging me as you say that," she said.

"I have never judged you, ever." I crossed my finger over the left side of my chest. "Cross my heart." She said nothing. "We're best friends, Jules. You can't leave me hanging like this."

The moment she opened her mouth to respond, the radio room door banged open and stopped us both. Luis stuck his head into the hallway. He looked tired, frazzled, and exhilarated.

"Boom, baby!" he yelled. "This radio station is open for business."

CHAPTER EIGHT

I stampeded into the room and left Jules in the corridor. Everyone crowded around the radio's crudely repaired casing. Circuitry and wiring still showed through gaps and a constant buzz of static emitted from the speaker. Marge was at the tuner and turned the dial with her skinny fingers, her head cocked to the side. Dan and his men stepped aside to make space for me beside her.

"This is awesome," I told her. "Thank you so, so much."

She smiled without taking her eyes off the display. "Oh, it was nothing, dear. You went to all that trouble to get me my things. The least I could do was use them. Here." She pushed her chair back. "You take over. I figure you must know what you're looking for better than I do."

"Uh, yeah." I stepped in front of the device and looked at the dials. "This thing will broadcast to other radios, won't it?"

"If they have a receiver, I don't see why not," said Marge.

My next question was the one that made me really

nervous. It hadn't occurred to me to ask while the radio was broken—I'd simply taken it for granted. "And how far will the signal go?"

"Hmm." She scratched her chin. "Well, this is shortwave radio we're talking about, which means skywave propagation. And it's a good one, military grade..." She faded off into indistinct mumbling about digital modes and finally returned. "I suppose you could hear overseas with it if you wanted to."

My heart jumped. "That's more than enough. I was worried about reaching California."

She barked a laugh. "California on this baby? Easy as pie. We might even be able to do it right now." She scooted in and manned the dials. "Assuming whoever you're trying to reach is listening, that is. The sun's not awake over there yet."

I cleared my throat. "Um, speaking of that, I'm sorry to have kept you up all night. I didn't know it would take this long."

She flapped a hand at me. "It's been years since I've had this kind of mental stimulation. If it takes me to an early grave, so be it."

The numbers on the digital readout cycled back and forth and the pitch of the static undulated. At moments of dead air, Marge stopped turning and picked up the microphone. "Hello?" she called. "Anyone out there?"

Five minutes stretched into ten, fifteen, and twenty. All of us except the old woman with the puffy hair held our breath and waited for a response. My high hopes flagged a little as we approached half an hour with no response.

Then the static skipped. Marge called out again. And a

voice eked out from behind the veil of static. "Yes, I read you. It's not very loud or clear, but I read you."

"Excellent!" Marge exclaimed jubilantly. "Who is this?"

"My name is N—" The voice cut out, stuttered and returned shakily. "Namiko. I'm in California, and I'm trying to—trying to reach s—someone."

"Namiko!" I practically shouted. I had known—or at least I had hoped—as soon as I saw the radio that I might be able to reach her on it. If anyone in the country had a working radio setup, it was probably her. The validation of my theory left me giddy with happiness and relief. "It's Vic! I'm here!" I was reasonably positive that the person she was trying to reach was me.

"Whoa," Namiko said. "No—no way. It finally worked."

"Finally?" I leaned forward. The static was so thick she was barely audible. "You've been trying to get through?"

"Only every day for—five weeks," she said. "Almost twenty-four-seven. I didn't even know if it was possible, but I guess it paid off." The static swelled briefly. "Listen, I don't—time to chat. We're not in the safest place, and we do what we can during the daylight, before the—comes out. I have to get going soon."

"Okay," I said. "Okay. Give me the quick rundown. How are things on the West Coast?"

"Could be better, could be worse," she said. "On the— hand, there are gods all the hell over the place, and they— not friendly. On the other, I'm linked up with a citizens' resistance—now, and we're getting shit done. When—can, anyway."

"Us too, sort of," I replied. "We're holed up in a fort with a big group, but I don't know how long it'll last."

"Groups are—all over the place," Namiko continued. "We're trying to band together to fight the gods. I've established a communications hub where I am so I can try to keep everyone updated. Leave your radio tuned to this frequency, okay? I broadcast every night when we're battened down."

"Do you know what gods are out there with you?" I asked.

"Not—much. Whoever it is, they've taken over a huge part of the Pacific Northwest. You know anything about Olympic National—"

"National what?" I leaned even closer as if that would help. Marge twisted the dial a fraction of an inch, and Namiko's garbled voice became slightly clearer.

"National Forest. They're living in it. It's huge. In Washington." There was a pause. "I was in contact with a girl from there for a while. Out by that area where the werewolves were, near Seattle. She said she knew you."

"Me?" I frowned.

"Yeah. Her name is Amber. She lives with her grandpa. He has a real old man name that I can't remember."

"Oh, shit! Amber and Smitty." I couldn't believe Namiko had been in touch with them. "Are they okay?"

"I don't know," Namiko said. "That's partially why I wanted to get in touch with you so badly. I last heard from Amber a while ago, and I think something's wrong. We had checked in daily before that."

"Oh, no." I ran my hand through my hair. What would I tell Maya? "Nothing from her at all?"

"Not a thing. I'm worried about her, and it extra sucks because she had a lot of information on those gods up there. They like the forest because they're some sort of tree people, is what she said. But she also mentioned fire a lot, which I feel doesn't really go with the forest thing?" Another pause. "Crap. I need to go soon. I have a name written down here somewhere." The static took over again, then abated. "Here! Oxfam? Oxtail? Oxy…lean? That's not right, but it's something like that."

"Thanks, Namiko," I said. "We'll figure it out. You get to safety. Take care of yourself."

"I'm fine," she said brightly. "No worries here. We'll be in touch."

"For sure. Over and out." I set the microphone down and straightened to stretch my back and shoulders. A strange well of emotion had opened in me on hearing Namiko's voice for the first time in ages, and I had to take a moment to shut it off. I turned to the team behind me who all awaited the next step. "Dan?" I asked.

He stepped forward, all business. "Here."

I looked at him. "Is there anyone you know who could get us across the country?"

CHAPTER NINE

I squinted blearily at the sunrise over the rim of a coffee cup and tried to focus on anything but the dull, no-sleep headache that percolated at my temples. The urge to close my eyes was incredible, but I'd lost my chance to sleep. Any minute now, Dan would return with a pilot. If all went according to plan, we'd be in the air shortly thereafter and wing our way toward Washington.

The decision hadn't been easy. All night, we stayed up and debated back and forth. Although I had wanted to go as soon as I heard Namiko's voice, I understood why someone might want to stay at the fort. And whether I liked it or not, someone would stay—a lot of people. Fort Victory was home to our tribe now. Whatever we did, we had to make sure the facility remained up and running.

There was no way around it. We would need to split up. I made the choice to go after Smitty simply because I refused to abandon him. That little Washington hamlet stood out in my mind's eye as clear as the day I first saw it. I remembered the old blacksmith and his strong-willed granddaughter and how they'd rallied behind me when I needed them. The way I saw it, to not go now would be nothing less than a betrayal.

I had to know what happened. Why did Amber and Namiko suddenly lose touch? I didn't know Amber extremely well, but she wasn't the type to abscond without a reason, especially in times like these. Namiko knew it too. If Amber's radio went dead, there was a huge problem. The thought of what we might walk into made shivers creep along my back and arms.

And we had already lost so much time.

I took a long sip of coffee and hoped the strong, dark elixir could inject some calm into my jittery nerves. It had been weeks, Namiko had said, since she'd last heard from Amber. She'd been stuck in California running her comms hub, or she probably would've traveled north herself. Frustrated that her hands were tied, she had instead focused on compiling all the data she received from Washington, the same intel she passed on to me.

"Marcus, are you awake?" I asked a little drowsily. "I think we should review." It was all information I had spent the past twelve hours scrutinizing in painstaking detail, but if nothing else, it would help me stay conscious.

Always. I no longer possess a biological need for sleep.

"Okay." I shook my head. "That's…weird. What do you do when—no, you know what? Some things should remain a mystery." I set the coffee cup down, leaned back in my chair, and once again resisted the powerful compulsion to allow my eyelids to droop until they shut. "Anyway, Namiko says this god near Amber and Smitty has taken over Olympic National Forest. Well, I had Dan look it up, and guess what? The land is freaking huge." I shuffled through the pad on which various notes were scribbled in my own sleep-deprived, barely legible hand. "Something like twenty-five hundred square kilometers. I'm not sure how much that is in miles, but it's still a lot."

I would call that a generally accurate statement, yes.

I stifled a giant yawn. "It makes me think there must be more than one holed up in there. We've never seen a single god dominate an area like that before. Not even Lorcan."

It is quite a formidable tract of territory, said Marcus. *We must assume its borders will be jealously guarded.*

"Yeah, of course," I agreed. "Whoever they are, they won't allow us to simply waltz in there and take it back. What I want to know is what we'll find. More werewolves maybe? A stronger kind?"

Lupres's influence may yet linger, but since he is dead, I strongly doubt his remaining followers could grow in power. It's more likely that this is a newcomer, one we have not yet seen. Your friend gave you a name, did she not? He paused. *Although I believe her pronunciation left much to be desired.*

"Oh, yeah." I passed a hand over my eyes. "Ox-something. Oxford. Oxbow. Oxygen?"

The Centurion chuckled. *I do know of a forest god named Oxylem. As for his powers, I cannot say for sure. His magic stretches back much further than many others. It is primitive in a way, ancient and wild. Its danger is not to be underestimated.*

I fished a pen from my pocket and scribbled on the bottom of the note page as I repeated aloud. "Oxylem—old as balls. Don't know what he does but can safely assume it sucks." I thought briefly. "Maybe it has something to do with fire. Namiko said Amber always talked about fire."

Marcus hesitated for a long minute. *I cannot say I understand that piece of the puzzle. I would think that, of all things, a forest god could be expected to avoid flames at all costs.*

"Or," I volunteered, "that's what he wants you to think. He might be a god of forest *fires.*"

No, said Marcus patiently. *Oxylem is not that. In fact, I cannot think of any flame wielders at all who could be associated with him. This is quite perplexing.*

"Well…" I frowned. "I guess it's always possible that Amber was mistaken." Even as I said the words, though, I knew I didn't believe them. Amber was too bullheaded and inquisitive not to have thoroughly investigated any strange occurrences. Hell, she'd likely gotten close enough to get her eyebrows singed. "I could've misunderstood Namiko, too. The radio connection wasn't great. I don't know." I ran both hands through my hair and blinked hard to keep the sleep away. "Where the hell is Dan? These three thousand miles won't traverse themselves."

He didn't show for another twenty minutes, time I used to consider who was grounded on the home team and who'd go away. I already had a rough idea of the squad compositions I wanted. The problem was that the arrangement in my head wouldn't be popular with everyone. I pinched the bridge of my nose as I did my best to anticipate reactions. I would've included everyone if it were feasible, but Fort Victory needed a few key personnel.

I was still hunched over, eyes scrunched shut as I rubbed my nose, when Dan walked in. "Bad time, chief?" he asked. "I've got good news if that helps."

I opened my eyes and glanced at him. "It's never a bad

time, Dan. I could use a morale booster. What have you got?"

At that point, I finally realized Dan wasn't alone. A squirrelly, ruddy man fidgeted intensely on his left. Sprigs of copper-colored hair catapulted from beneath a worn-out woolen beanie. The man's iridescent green eyes bugged in their sockets. He shifted his weight constantly from one foot to the other.

Dan gestured to the guy. "I'd like to introduce you to our new ace pilot."

A wide, misshapen grin spread rapidly across the man's face. He stuck his hand out to me but still moved back and forth. Even our handshake felt restless. "Call me Ginger," he declared enthusiastically. "Better'n any other name I got."

I raised an eyebrow at Dan. "Where'd you find this one?"

He shrugged. "I pulled him from the group in the tunnel after you took down the one with the bull's horns back in New York City. I'm not sure what he has left in terms of common sense, but he swears up and down that he can fly whatever we need him to."

Ginger nodded resolutely. "Anything. If it's got wings, you put me in that cockpit, and I'll get it off the ground." He offered his hand for another shake. "Want to see my license? I've got it right here." His bulbous eyes fastened on my face.

This man is very odd, perhaps untrustworthy, Marcus commented in my ear. *What is this license he speaks of?*

Despite Marcus's skepticism, Ginger pulled out a faded leather wallet and produced a blue-green card from within the pocket. The ID was emblazoned with a crest I didn't recognize, and it listed his name as Henry E. Dobbson, certified for commercial and private flight. I looked at the man. He stood and watched me while he smiled broadly and continued that irritating rocking. "Hasn't even expired yet," he said proudly.

Dan cleared his throat. "I'm willing to vouch for our friend here, Vic," he said and clapped the hyperactive man on the shoulder. Ginger, caught off guard, almost buckled to the floor. The soldier turned to him. "Why don't you tell Vic what you found?"

"What I found?" An expression of pure bemusement skated across Ginger's face and lingered for a moment before it cleared once again into that wide grin. "Oh! Oh, yes. Yes. I found a plane."

My jaw fell open. "What?" I had assumed we'd have to steal one or that Dan had a special contact we could reach now that we had a working radio. "How do you simply find a damn plane?"

Ginger raised his brows and opened his green eyes wide. "I like to walk, y'see? In my free time, which I have a lot of these days, I walk. And one day, I walked around behind that place." He pointed toward the dungeon. "Nobody goes there on account of it being so close to where the bodies were."

I winced. We'd done our best to shelter the general populace from that particularly ugly truth, but there was no way to hide the procession of corpses that had to be removed. "Go on," I prompted, eager to change the subject. "That's where the plane is?"

"I tell you, I was as shocked as you are now." Ginger

threw up his freckled hands. "Another building. Who woulda thunk?" He leaned in. "But it's pretty small for a hangar. You can't see it from the front side, so I don't want you feeling bad."

"Thanks. Did you see the plane?" My impatience bubbled beneath the surface. I wanted to grab the pilot by the collar and shake him until all the relevant words fell out but I held back. He didn't seem like he was all there, at least not all the time.

"Sure, I did. Big old honkin' padlocks on the doors, but there's a window right in front. Now, I gotta warn you…" His face became somber. "She's small, this bird. Not a lot of room for warm bodies, if you know what I'm saying." He flicked his gaze between Dan and me as if he counted in his head. "I bet we could squeeze in a bunch of passengers if you're willing to get cozy."

"We'll manage," I said. I wouldn't have cared if he made me sit in the plane's cargo hold, as long as it got me to Washington. "Jules and Veronica are getting provisions ready as we speak."

"That leaves only one thing," Dan declared. "Who gets the four mission slots?" He instantly rephrased. "Three, that is, alongside our illustrious leader."

I chewed my lip as I looked at him. "Don't hate me, Dan. But can I ask you to stay?" Before he had a chance to protest, I rushed on. "The fort needs someone to head up its defenses, and there's no one I trust more in that department than you. It's a critical role. I need you to make sure Fort Victory's still here when we get back."

At first, his normally jovial face remained completely flat and expressionless. I was about to launch into another attempt to convince him when his usual big smile made an appearance. "I'd be glad to, Vic," he said. "Don't you worry a thing about it. You know you can count on me."

I heaved a huge sigh of relief. "Thank you so much, man. I think Jules and Veronica need to be here to keep the supply system going, and…" My heart sank. "I'll put Maya in charge."

"It'll be fine," Dan said reassuringly. "Maya's great. Everyone loves her. You couldn't pick a better stand-in."

"I know." I glanced toward the residential wing where I knew she had hurried off to her room after our all-nighter meeting ended. "I only hope she sees it that way too."

CHAPTER TEN

I dragged my feet a little bit on my way to Maya's room, reluctant to be the bearer of devastating news. To the best of my knowledge, she had never really been mad at me, and I didn't want to break that streak of good fortune. During our debate the previous night, she had sided with me in no uncertain terms about going to Washington immediately. She had also expected to be part of that deployment.

To be told otherwise might break her heart.

While I hated to be the one to do that to her, it couldn't be anyone else. In the beginning, when she was still uncertain and learning, I'd been the one to boost her confidence and tell her she was valuable and cool. Now, I had to tell her she was needed more at home than she was in the field, that she had to be Maya for a while, not Were-Maya. Strangely, I felt unprepared for a conversation like that.

I paused in the hallway to psyche myself up. "You can do this, Vic," I murmured. "She'll understand. Be honest.

Tell her how important this is and how much you believe in her. God, I hope this works."

"Hey, Vic." The smooth, deep voice made me jump as I turned, my body poised for flight even though I knew automatically who it was. Deacon looked at me a little puzzled and a smile tilted his lips. "I didn't mean to scare you. How are you holding up?"

I laughed it off. "Oh, you know me. Always lost in thought. I'm actually doing pretty damn well, all things considered. I feel good about this whole thing." I gestured to the fort around me. "We've built this place up, and we've kicked major ass. I *am* nervous about where Smitty and Amber are, but there's nothing we can do about that until we get there." I gazed at him with a smile. "Yeah. Things are good. We're good."

Deacon chuckled. "You're something else, girl. For real." He stepped closer and rested a hand on my arm. Somehow, even the scent of the plain military soap was sexy emanating from his body. Our eyes locked. "I like spending time with you when we're not getting shot at."

"Real smooth, Barry White," I said. "Me too. It almost makes me feel bad about being so suspicious of you when we first met."

He laughed. "To be fair, you had every reason to be. And you were right." He squeezed my arm gently. "I was on your case that whole damn time."

I grinned. "You sly dog. Lucky for me, you were no match for my show-stopping looks and sparkling personality."

Deacon shifted even closer. "I'd say it was more your strength in the face of adversity, your badass nature, and your sharp mind and sharper wit." He smirked. "And those amazing eyes."

I leaned away from him and folded my arms. "You didn't even mention my ass."

Another laugh rumbled from his chest. "Do I really need to?"

His full lips curled in a charming smile and his eyes twinkled with endless possibilities. It was my turn to step in closer and onto the tips of my toes. This moment had been a long time coming, maybe even since that night at Jules's party.

We both felt it.

Deacon's hands rested lightly on my waist. His face drew closer. I started to close my eyes, not wanting to see but simply to feel.

Someone coughed behind us.

The romantic moment shattered into a million pieces. "Damn it," I said out loud. I turned to see Luis standing there with a sheepish grin on his face.

"Sorry," he said. "I'd say I can come back later, but we gotta get a move on if we want to get out of here. I need to borrow your man for some prep. Promise you'll get him back in one piece."

"He's not the one I'm worried about," I replied.

Luis clapped a hand over his heart as if he'd been shot and pretended to fold back onto the tile. "Damn, Vic. Words hurt, you know?"

Deacon slipped by me. "I'll take a rain check," he said softly. Then, to Luis, he said, "All right, man. You and me against the world."

"With you on my team?" Luis asked. "My money's on the world."

I shook my head and resumed my trek toward Maya's room. The warmth of Deacon's touch still radiated through my body and melted away some of my stress. I stopped with my hand on her door and inhaled deeply. I could hear her moving around on the other side. A zipper closed.

"Maya?" I knocked lightly. "It's Vic. Can I come in?"

"It's open," she called back.

I turned the handle and walked inside. The scene before me was as I feared. Maya packed a bag frantically in preparation for an unexpected but now highly anticipated trip to the community she had left behind.

"Hey," I said and glanced at her stuff. "Listen, I know you're getting ready to leave, but...I'm here to ask you to take over the fort while I'm gone."

Maya stopped dead and dropped her bundle of toiletries onto the mattress. "What?" She rotated slowly to face me. "You're joking, right?"

I shook my head apologetically. "I want to know the place is in good hands. Yours are the best we've got."

She pressed her lips together. "Those are my people in Washington, Vic. I need to go. I need to help them." A note of desperation colored her voice and flared in her eyes. "I can't sit here and do nothing." She sat down on the edge of the bed next to her toiletry kit, stunned.

I crossed the small room to sit beside her. "Maya, you won't be doing nothing. I understand that Washington was your home before we met, but since then, you've made a home for more than a hundred refugees here. These are your people now. They're the ones who need you the most." I put my hand on her back. "Smitty and Amber can take care of themselves. You know that better than anyone. And once we find them, they'll take care of their community like I'm sure they've done all along."

"I know," Maya said quietly. "But I wanted…" She trailed off glumly. I slipped my arm around her shoulder.

"It's not that I don't want you to come with me," I told her. "You're a beast out there, and I mean that on every conceivable level. You can stomp a vamp into the ground and turn and fix up the poor sucker he was trying to kill. And on top of that, you're a born leader."

Her eyes narrowed in thought. "I never considered myself a leader."

"Well, you are," I said. "And that's why I need you stationed here. Who else can handle the fort like you can? Who will pull double duty as the doctor and as the first line of defense if something happens? I can't do this mission while I look over my shoulder to make sure everything's kosher at home. You're the only one I trust to do that for me."

"Aw, shucks," she said and grinned. "I bet you say that to all your underlings."

"I *did* say it to Dan," I admitted. "In my defense, I was only talking about security. You're the one who's in charge, and he knows it. Also, you're not my underling. I'm lucky to be your equal and your friend."

"Whoa, there." Maya gave me a quick hug. "I think we all know who's the real boss here." She put on a brave face. "Okay. I'll steer the ship. Say hi to Smitty and Amber for me, will you?"

"Dude, of course. We'll make sure we get their radio in working order so we can talk to them whenever we want."

"That would be so great. Thanks, Vic." Maya's expression hardened with determination. "I promise I won't let you down."

With renewed purpose, she unpacked her bag and put things in their proper place.

I stood. "I know you won't. I wouldn't be here without you. You're a beast."

"Ha ha." She gave me a look. "Get going, boss. The home front will be fine."

I grinned. "Atta girl."

CHAPTER ELEVEN

The sun still straggled up the eastern face of the morning sky as our away team marched toward the makeshift hangar at the back of the sprawling property. Deacon, Brax and I headed the small battalion. Luis trailed behind us, and a choice selection of Dan's men and the best newly trained fighters brought up the rear.

"Vic is the ultimate authority on this mission," Dan had said to his men and to the trainees. "She is the alpha and the omega, you understand? She says jump, you ask how high."

"Sir, yes, sir!" was the response. It had been a concern of mine that the refugees—a lot of whom were in similar situations to Luis—would rebel against the kind of structured training we put them through, but they seemed to thrive on it instead. I assumed the strength of our common enemy was enough to calm the intrinsic fires of youth.

Up close, the hangar was ramshackle and so was the plane it housed within its single bay. I appraised the craft for a few moments and did my absolute best to hide the creeping doubt in the pit of my stomach. Luis, on the other hand, didn't even make the effort.

"We're *flying* in that piece of shit?" he burst out. Some of the soldiers snorted. Luis was unfazed. "It doesn't look like you could even drive that thing."

Ginger appeared behind him like a wild-eyed ghost. "Oh, you can. I mean, *you* can't. But I can." He trotted ahead of the group toward the plane. The doors were still heavily padlocked.

"Who the hell hired this guy?" Brax grumbled.

I glanced at him. While I itched to ask where he'd run off to, I knew better than to expect an answer. The demon had been more or less MIA since I had seen him with Jules in the classroom, and I wasn't even sure if he'd show up again at the right time.

But he had and now, he pulled his great hammer off his back. "Whatever," he said brusquely and strode behind the pilot. "I'll take care of this shit. Stand back. Way back."

Ginger was too confused to act fast, and he hesitated too long. In the next second, he had to fend off a shower of sparks. Brax's hammer turned the first lock into a twisted, glowing mass. He reared back to strike again, and Ginger skedaddled to a safe distance with wide eyes.

We were certainly some kind of motley crew.

Brax kicked both broken locks off, extinguished his hammer, and put it away in one smooth motion. "There," he said and brushed his hands off. "Don't say I never did anything for you."

Truly, he is a paragon of virtue. Marcus's voice dripped with sarcasm. I wondered if he'd be that sassy for the rest of the mission. Sassy Marcus was always a lot of fun.

"Thank you, Brax," I said and maneuvered around him to reach the plane. Without a grimy pane of glass between us, the aircraft seemed even more impossibly rickety and in bad condition. Paint peeled off its hull. I thought I saw a crack in the windshield. "Hey, Ginger. Are you sure this thing is, uh, air-safe?"

"Nope," Ginger responded cheerfully. "But I can fly it." He tugged at the door, which came loose with a puff of dust. Cobwebs hung from the handle.

I looked at Deacon. "I don't know if this is such a good idea after all. I mean, I want to get to Washington like crazy, but I'd like to get there alive."

"That's funny," the FBI agent said. "I thought the same thing." Ahead of us, Ginger climbed into the plane and disappeared inside the cockpit.

My mind raced to come up with a solution. "Dan's got access to satellite maps, doesn't he? Maybe we could find an airport. There must be one reasonably close to here, right?" It was a shot in the dark, but it was the best shot we had. No way would we get to Washington without a plane.

Brax emitted a tortured groan. "You humans are assholes," he said. "I'll go tell what's-his-nuts we need the map." With that, he turned and stomped toward the fort.

"Did he volunteer to do something?" Deacon asked, genuinely curious.

I nodded. "Yeah. It was weird." I kept my eyes trained on the demon's receding figure as he approached the front of the fort. It was so unlike him to go out of his way to do anything. I had a sneaking suspicion what he was up to.

Sure enough, a blonde shape I could've identified in whiteout conditions met him on the lawn. They interacted for only a second, but it was long enough for me to see her hand him something. He slipped it into his long black coat. Jules turned and walked inside with him.

"What the fuck?" I whispered.

Deacon glanced at me, his brow furrowed. "What are you talking about?"

"You missed that whole thing?" I asked.

"What thing?"

I sighed heavily. "Never mind." It was probably me being paranoid and making things up where they didn't exist. Jules had no reason to befriend a demon, let alone anything more than that. Besides, I knew Brax totally wasn't her type.

Still, what did she give him? I really wanted to know. The thought gnawed at my brain until he got back with the satellite mapping device in hand. I had to force myself not to look directly at his coat pocket.

"Here." He thrust the device into my hand. "You're welcome."

Deacon came to look over my shoulder and we studied the screen together. I zoomed it out so we could see miles in every direction. "What's that?" He pointed to a large open area with a few strips of tarmac running through it. I focused in on it.

"It looks like a private airstrip," I said. "It'll do." I waved to our assembled group. "Get to the trucks, you guys. We'll take a little road trip."

I turned to Brax. "Could you take this b—"

"He said to keep it," Brax interrupted in a tone that suggested I might be the dumbest jackass on the planet. "I guess he has another one." He walked away before he finished his last sentence and left me with Deacon behind our mobilizing troops.

"Is it just me, or is he stiffer than usual?" Deacon remarked.

"It's not you," I muttered. "Let's go." I was so focused on Brax that I almost didn't notice Ginger still in the hangar. He clambered around under the control panels in the cockpit.

"Henry!" I yelled.

His head popped up. "Don't call me that."

"Didn't you hear me?" I motioned toward the rest of the squad. "We're leaving. Come on."

"I thought we were leaving in this." He looked at me as though all his dreams had been crushed. "I told you I can fly it."

"And I believe you." I stopped and looked from him to my retreating battalion. "But you've messed around in there for a while now, and it looks like it'll fall apart before we reach cruising altitude. We'll go to a real airstrip instead."

He brightened immediately. "Why didn't you say so?" Like a creepy leprechaun, he hopped out of the plane and scurried past us, whistling atonally as he went. "I'll have my pick of whatever I want. Rich people's planes, I hope. Oh, I hope!"

"Every time I think this situation can't get weirder." Deacon touched my back. The heat of his hand seemed to penetrate all my layers of clothing. "Let's catch up before that crazy loon gets behind the wheel."

"What do you think the odds of him actually being able

to fly a plane are?" I wondered out loud. We broke into a jog after everyone else.

"How honest do you want me to be?" he asked.

I smirked. "Totally."

He cast a worried glance at the back of Ginger's head. "Ten to one," he said. "Against us."

CHAPTER TWELVE

Deacon and I split up to drive the trucks out of the fort complex. I took Luis in my passenger seat, and as we moved down the long path to the road, I glanced in the rearview mirror. Ginger had declined a seat in Deacon's vehicle. I could see him lean out from the truck bed and grin in the open air. The sight didn't exactly fill me with confidence.

The ride to the airstrip proved to be uneventful, which was a small consolation. The gate into the main area was already busted open when we got there. It hung on its hinges and the chain dangled freely. "Keep your eyes open," I told Luis.

"No worries," he answered. "I stopped closing them a long time ago."

The airstrip was mostly comprised of a cluster of low buildings overshadowed by a lone control tower. All the windows were dark and empty. The field itself looked barren, and a couple of small planes stood in the open. I heard an enthusiastic whoop from behind us, and a redheaded streak raced past the window. I rubbed my face. "So much for a stealthy approach."

Ginger tore across the grass with surprising vigor. At the edge of the first runway, he stopped dead and scanned the place like a human antenna. I turned our truck off and got out. The others did the same. We stood a few dozen yards behind the pilot and watched him take stock.

"What the hell is he doing?" Deacon asked. "I thought he was gonna break his neck when he jumped off the truck. That guy's a real piece of work."

"He's all we've got," I said. "I think he's choosing our ride."

Deacon's eyes suddenly snapped to stare far down the airfield toward the edge of the property. "He better get a move on. Look." He pointed, and I caught sight of a familiar group of ragged monsters racing directly toward us.

"Uh oh. Hey, Ginge! Pick up the pace, would you? We've got company." I motioned for the whole squad to prepare. The gap between this band of Forgotten and us was closing faster than I would have liked. I could see them clearly now—a mismatched crew of mostly vamps, centaurs, and satyrs. As rowdy as ever, the satyrs shouted, discharged guns in the air, and made obscene gestures with their free hands.

Luis groaned. "I have had it with these fucking jokers," he declared and leveled his rifle. The first volley of fire rang through the air.

"Seriously, Ginger!" I yelled over the noise. "Any time you're ready."

He glanced over his shoulder as if he'd only now

noticed the enemy, and his eyes went wide. "Okay. Okay." He spun and sprinted for a mid-sized craft. His voice trailed behind him. "Cover me while I steal this thing."

It wasn't like we had much of a choice. I plunged into the fray and sliced through a vamp and two satyrs in quick succession. The combination of the centaurs' pounding hooves and the dust from the dead vamps churned the air into a haze. Some of the newly trained soldiers coughed.

"Try not to breathe that," I advised them and dropped another enemy at my feet. "It's basically corpse dust. I have no idea what it'll do to your lungs." They gave me horrified glances, and one of them gagged. "Hey, I'm trying to help you out."

As far as I know, expired vampires are not a significant source of toxicity. I am not, however, an expert on the intricacies of Forgotten biology.

"We'll notify the FDA," I said. "Maybe they'll label these assholes a health risk." I shot a look over my shoulder to monitor Ginger's progress. The door to the plane was open, and I thought I saw one of his feet hanging out. To Deacon, I shouted, "Start moving toward the plane, and get ready to run for it the second he gives the signal."

He nodded, and we shepherded the fight carefully toward our escape aircraft but made sure to maintain a barrier between the pilot and us. The Forgotten didn't seem to care too much about whether we tried to get away. They merely wanted to kill us.

Some of them looked like they wanted to eat us.

The beasts clearly weren't immune to the effects of having to scavenge for food. The group was scrawny and pale, and some of the satyrs were missing patches of hair on their hoofed legs. A centaur lay near me, bleeding from the flank, and his ribcage was little more than hide stretched over bones.

They had battle scars too—whether from infighting or run-ins with other survivors, I couldn't be sure. Lucky for us, they were easily dispatched in their weakened state. I fell back toward Ginger as Luis and the others picked off the last of the stragglers.

"Let's go, you guys!" I made sure the pilot could hear me, too. "Grab whatever you left in the trucks and get your asses over here." The last sentence was punctuated by a grumbling roar as the plane's engine came to life. "That's our cue. Time to hit the road. Or hit the sky, I guess."

"As long as we don't hit the ground," Deacon said beside me where he watched my flank.

"Amen to that," I said.

My men ran across the tarmac with their stuff slung over their shoulders. From the cockpit, Ginger yelled triumphantly. "We're in business, ladies and gents."

I stood back so everyone else could pile in first, which was how I saw the second group of Forgotten come around the corner of the control tower. The centaurs at the front broke into a frenzied gallop and leveled their gleaming weapons in our direction.

"Go!" I pushed the last few passengers up the stairs and through the doorway before I followed them inside. The door clanged shut behind me. I called into the cockpit, "Go now! We're out of time."

"Roger that!" Ginger hollered back. "Please fasten your seatbelts. This is a nonsmoking flight." He shrugged. "I mean that hopefully, nothing starts smoking."

The plane rolled forward along the runway and gradually picked up speed. I made my way to the rearmost window and gazed at the pack of monsters that hounded us. The satyrs had more or less fallen away, but the vamps and centaurs had gained. Their eyes stared at us with a feral, hungry glint.

Those guys *definitely* wanted to eat us.

"Step on it, Ginger!" I yelled.

"That's not really how this works," he yelled back, but the rumble of the engine intensified. The scenery through the window began to blur. As I felt us lift off the ground, the lead vamp lunged forward and became airborne himself.

I lost sight of him. "Oh, shit."

A loud, scraping thump drowned out the curse.

"We're off balance," Ginger said. "What's going on out there?"

I moved to check another window and came face to face with the damn vamp who now clung to the wing. The airflow swept his hair and skin taut against his skull, and his tattered clothes threatened to abandon him entirely.

Brax loomed over my shoulder. "I got this one," he said flatly. Before I could react, he strode to the exit, pushed it open, and disappeared into the howling wind.

Common sense continues to be one of Abraxzael's weaker attributes, Marcus remarked.

"Whatever he's doing, I hope he does it quick," Deacon said while he struggled to secure the door. "If we're too high when he opens that door again, the whole cabin will depressurize."

"Don't say that shit out loud," Luis hissed. He gripped

the arms of his seat with both hands, his knuckles white. "It's bad luck."

"Facts don't have anything to do with luck," the agent retorted, but he kept quiet after that.

Brax entered the window's field of vision, half bent against the wind as he made his way toward the vamp. His coat whipped ferociously around his solid frame like a dark aura. They painted a surreal picture as they faced each other on the wing, poised to do battle.

"Yo, he looks pretty dope," said one of the soldiers. "I hope he smokes this dude."

I could go either way, Marcus said.

"Be nice," I said softly.

Fine. I hope the demon is merely wounded.

"See? Was that so hard?"

Extremely.

I shook my head and turned my attention to the fight.

The vamp lashed out first, but it immediately scrabbled for a handhold so it wouldn't fly off onto the tarmac. Brax, perpetually unimpressed, loosed his hammer from its holster on his back. He couldn't light it out there, but it still packed a mean punch. Steadying himself as best he could, he swung.

The vamp flattened on the wing and hissed, its fangs bared. It tried to grab the demon's leg, but he kicked and landed his boot square in the middle of the vampire's face. It barely managed to evade his next hammer strike, at which point Brax, clearly frustrated, put the hammer on his back and leaned forward to grab his foe. He lifted the skinny creature by the front of its shirt. Although it struggled desperately and clawed at his arms, he carried it to the edge of the wing and dropped it into oblivion.

Such crude tactics, Marcus said. *No finesse. No sophistication.*

"He could've danced a ballet out there and you'd still say that," I muttered.

And I would be correct. We are lucky he did not pummel the wing right off the plane.

The exit door opened again and blasted us with freezing air. Brax stepped inside, slammed it shut, and proceeded to stare down everyone who looked at him.

"What do you want?" he demanded. "Problem solved." The discussion over, he walked down the aisle to a seat by a window, sat, and whipped out his sunglasses.

CHAPTER THIRTEEN

I sat in the back row of the plane with Deacon, spread out over two seats with the armrests up. He rested one arm casually over my knee and had been quiet since the incident on the wing. The view outside wasn't much more than a wet-looking mat of gray, and he sat facing the front. His dark eyes were thoughtful.

"Can I ask you something?" he asked suddenly. "About earlier?"

I glanced at him and thought about that moment in the hall and how close we'd come to acting on long-held mutual desires. "Here?" I asked. "This is kind of a weird place to finish what we started, don't you think? I mean, we're surrounded by soldiers." I paused. "Unless you're into that."

"What?" He held his palms up to stop me. "No. It's actually kind of the opposite." He paused. "I wondered about where Marcus fits into things like this. Since, you know, he's always around."

I raised an eyebrow. "Spit it out, St. Clare. What are you trying to say?"

Deacon sighed. Somewhat sheepishly, he said, "Does he hear everything?"

I glanced at the medallion and snorted. "That's what you're worried about? Of course, he doesn't. We have an agreement."

He didn't seem convinced. "Which is what?" he pressed.

"Think of it as a mute button," I said. "Whatever I don't want him to hear, he doesn't hear. He can also close himself off from having to listen to what's going on over here, and I'm sure he does that at least occasionally."

"And you trust him about this?" Deacon still looked a little worried. "I don't mean to disrespect the guy. But I can't see him, and you always talk to him, so..." He shrugged. "I wanted to know how it works, so I can hopefully not embarrass myself too badly. If I haven't already."

Tell him to fear not. My integrity is beyond repute. I have afforded you every privacy in the past, and you may rest assured I will continue to do so. Also, tell him he has indeed already embarrassed himself.

I suppressed a smile and patted Deacon's hand. "Marcus is totally a stand-up guy. Some would say he's got a boner for honor."

*Who says that? Identify the slanderer and allow me to redeem my—*Marcus stopped.

I grinned. "You were gonna say 'honor,' weren't you?"

He answered with silence.

"Marcus is fine," I said to my companion. "Besides, if I ever really wanted to make sure he was out of the loop, I could simply take the medallion off."

Visible relief passed over Deacon's features. "Oh, you can do that? I'm not gonna lie, that makes me feel a lot better."

I smirked. "How come? We've hardly done anything that would require that level of discretion. If I didn't know any better, I'd say you were angling for—"

The plane bumped in the air and my words cut off as I lurched forward. Deacon caught my legs in time to avoid being kneed in the face. We braced against the seats in front of us and looked at each other.

The cabin's intercom clicked on. "Sorry about that, folks," Ginger announced. "We're experiencing some routine turbulence. Well, it's not that routine, actually. We're heading for a fairly big storm, and I don't think it'll move out of the way anytime soon. Things are about to get fun."

He clicked off. The aircraft shuddered again. It took an abrupt dip, and I felt my stomach lift into freefall for a second.

"Hey, whoa, I'm not into this," Luis said. His face had gone as pale as a sheet. The soldier beside him nudged him in the ribs.

"First time flying?" he asked.

"And probably the last if it's always like this." Luis closed his eyes as the plane bucked once more.

"Don't sweat it," the soldier said. "Let me show you how to assume the crash position."

"*Dios mio*," Luis muttered. He clutched his grandmother's rosary. I felt a little sorry for him.

Five minutes later, the plane rattled like it was about to burst into pieces. The tossing sensation was so intense, we might as well have been on the ocean. Our loose bags tumbled through the cabin. I caught mine on its way down the aisle and buckled it into an empty seat.

The door to the cockpit opened. "I have some bad news." Ginger was obviously stressed and had worked his red hair into a crazy poof with nervous fingers. "I'm afraid we'll have to land. The storm's not going away, and we can't keep going through this." His laugh sounded strained. "Even I'm not nuts enough for that. Not with you all in the plane, anyway."

Luis spoke through clenched teeth and still clutched the rosary. "Look, man, I don't care what you have to do as long as you get the hell back to the freaking controls. I know there's no copilot in there."

"The plane has an automatic pilot," Ginger said. He tapped a finger to his lips. "Although I don't think I turned it on."

"Please, just fly the goddamn plane!" Luis said.

Ginger jumped. "Right. Right! Sorry." He disappeared into the cockpit and emerged a second later. "I probably should have simply used the intercom."

"Fly the fucking plane!" Luis yelled.

Ginger nodded and squirreled himself away into the front of the aircraft.

"Shit, I should have asked him where we are," I said. It was hard to have a sense of time up there, but I thought we'd flown for a few hours at least. "We'd better be ready for anything."

"Aren't we always?" Deacon asked.

The landing was fast and rough. We definitely weren't at an airport. A couple of times during the hurried descent,

I had to stop my doubts as to whether Ginger could pull this off. We shoved through the bottom layer of clouds, and the world came into view much closer than I had expected. Fortunately, everything below us appeared to be unrelentingly flat, checkered farmland.

Deacon stared out the window. "Based on that panorama, I'd say we're somewhere in the Midwest."

He turned out to be right. The plane cut through an abandoned cornfield, where we waited for the storm to pass. About an hour in, we were accosted by a herd of warty toad-people who'd lost their ability to speak in anything other than croaks, grunts, and gurgles. Although I stayed vigilant, there was no sign of a toad god, and for that, I was eternally grateful. Even Marcus had been mystified by them. He wasn't able to identify a deity with matching or similar characteristics.

Perhaps, he had mused, *the gods are changing. Or perhaps they are more numerous and varied than I have known.*

None of it boded well for our troop of explorers, and we got the hell out of Dodge the instant the thunder and lightning cleared up. Ginger managed to coax us back into the air despite the lack of a proper runway or any sort of guiding lights. Somewhat apprehensively, I settled in to try to relax for the rest of the flight, hoping the drama was behind us.

It wasn't.

Some two hours later, a great impact rocked the side of the plane and jerked me violently out of a fitful nap. I gasped and bolted upright. "What the fuck was that?"

"More bad news," Ginger said over the intercom. There was little levity left in his voice. He cleared his throat. "The display up here tells me one of the engines blew. And that means we are in for the crash landing of a lifetime."

The soldier next to Luis laughed nervously. "Hey, remember how I was going to show you how to do the crash position?"

"I thought you were joking," Luis exclaimed.

"Well, I was at the time," he said. "Now, I'm not."

The plane rolled forward and tipped sharply downward. The sensation was a little like a roller coaster, only infinitely more terrifying because I had a fairly good idea of how high up we were. Once more, my stomach floated up, and this time, it stayed there for what seemed like forever. The uneven thrum of the engine sounded worse and worse in my ears. Beneath it all, I heard Luis reciting something in Spanish.

Probably a prayer.

I put my head down between my arms and stared at the floor in front of my seat. Aside from the chugging engine and Luis's panicked appeal, the cabin was as silent as it could get. We hardly breathed. Outside, the land drew closer and closer.

The plane leveled out. My stomach settled back into place. I didn't dare release my grip until it was down, but it took only a few more seconds for the wheels to hit solid ground.

Luis yelped. The brake flaps on the wings popped open. We still hurtled forward at breakneck speed, but we gradually slowed. The last sound to die was the broken engine. After that, nothing moved—including us.

"Is it over?" Luis asked. "Am I fucking dead, or what?"

The soldier beside him was the first to laugh, and it

spread from person to person like a joyful epidemic. Even Brax chuckled. Ginger emerged from the cockpit to a miniature celebration and a round of applause.

"Sorry I yelled at you before, *hermano*," Luis apologized. "You really pulled it through for us."

The pilot grinned, and his freckled cheeks flushed. "To be fair, I really should have used the intercom."

We all exited the plane. The air on the other side of the door was fresh, rain-scented, and twenty degrees warmer than it had been when we left. Droplets of condensation clung to my skin and hair as I stood and examined the satellite device. We'd touched down not far from the edge of a thick, imposing forest, which I hoped might be the one we were looking for.

A ping from the GPS confirmed it. We stood outside Olympic National Forest, only a few miles from our target destination.

"That was some good flying," I said to Ginger. "And some good navigating, to boot."

"Thank you." He beamed for a moment until the grin fell from his face. "Please don't make me go out there. I told you I can fly, and I proved it. But I can't do anything else. And I need to fix this baby, so we'll be able to leave when the time comes." He shifted anxiously from foot to foot.

"No problem," I said quickly. "We'll leave you with a guard so you can do your job. And a gun, in case you need to defend yourself." I retrieved a handgun from one of the bags and gave it to him. He held it awkwardly as if it might explode.

"A gun," he said warily. "Okay. Yes. Thank you. I won't use it."

"With any luck, you won't have to make that choice," I said. I moved to gather up the rest of my squadron. By some miracle of faith and Ginger's piloting, everyone had walked away from that landing unscathed, if a little spooked. They all seemed grateful to do something as mundane as form up, and the pair I tasked with watching Ginger's back stationed themselves outside the downed craft without complaint.

The rest of us marched out and advanced into the cover of towering trees.

CHAPTER FOURTEEN

Beyond the first few hundred feet, the woods weren't as thick as they looked from the outside. The evidence of raging forest fires soon appeared, stark and unmistakably harrowing. Ashy husks of tree trunks, some still adorned with skeletal branches, flanked each side of the narrow path we followed. The sound of raindrops dripping from dead trees surrounded our party.

"This place is as spooky as shit," a soldier remarked and turned almost three hundred and sixty degrees to avoid leaving himself with any blind spots. "You said there are *gods* in here?"

"There's one," I said. "And our job is to find him."

We walked in single file, but the guys clumped together and held their weapons tightly, their heads virtually on swivels. Brax, Deacon, and I kept our cool. Every now and then, I glanced at the satellite map to make sure we were still on track. The remains of campsites lay among the trees with scattered belongings mostly ruined by prolonged exposure to the elements. A few of the tents had long tears raked into the sides.

"I'd hate to find out what did that," Deacon murmured.

Brax grunted. "I have a feeling we will, whether we like it or not." He had moved up to lead with us at the front. "I don't see any bodies, though, so people either got out themselves or were taken away."

"I hope it's the former," I said.

He didn't look at me when he said, "Yeah. Me too."

The demon is ill, Marcus interjected. *Something in his brain has misfired and created a kernel of compassion.*

"Tell your invisible buddy to shut his trap," said Brax. "I can't hear him, but I know he's talking, and I know it's about me. Maybe he ought to worry about himself for a change."

I have nothing to worry about. My every action is blessed with honor.

I pursed my lips. "I'll pass it on."

"Good." The demon moved slightly ahead of us and his dark-clad shape almost blended into the gloom. I used the dull gleam of the hammer to keep track of him as the shadows deepened. A thick, impenetrable blanket of quiet dropped over us. With a jolt, I realized I could no longer see the sun.

"Hold up," I called softly. Brax stopped and half-turned toward me. "Something's screwy here. Why's it so dark?" I retrieved the GPS unit and focused on the screen, but it took an awfully long time to locate a signal.

"Where are we?" Luis looked at the canopy of branches and hushed pine. "Don't tell me we're lost, Vic. This is like nature's version of a graveyard."

"We can't be lost," I said. "I've followed the route on the map exactly. If we're wrong, then everything's wrong."

"That's not helpful," he replied. He was still recovering from the plane adventure earlier, and his normally level head was a little off-kilter. "This freaks me out, man. If we go any farther in, we won't come out."

"That's not true." I went to him and put my hands on his shoulders. "Look at me, Luis. In the eye. I know this trip has been tough for you so far, but I need you to pull yourself together. I brought you along because you're strong and smart and you know what you're doing. Take a deep breath. Shut your brain off for a minute if you have to. I'm depending on you to be here in the moment."

The kid stared at me and for a second, I didn't think my words had taken hold. Then he sucked in a deep breath, held it, and blew it out. Some of the scared emptiness left his big brown eyes. He had never looked younger.

"Okay," he said. He shook his head. "Okay. I got you. I'm good."

"You sure?" I gave his shoulders a gentle shake. "Because I'm about to give you marching orders, and I have to know you can carry them out."

"No...yeah." Now, Luis nodded and tried his best to grin. It wasn't as solid as usual, but better than before. "I just—I think the plane thing kinda messed with me, is all. I'm fine. What do you want me to do?"

I squeezed his shoulder. "Glad to have you back. Deacon, Brax, and I will do a little recon. I want you to stay here with the troops until we get back. Don't let anyone move. Don't let anyone leave. If something happens, give us a shout." I pointed to the radio on his chest. "We'll be back soon."

"Good luck," he said and saluted.

"You guys hear that?" I asked the others. "Luis is in charge right now. Don't make his life difficult." They were too unsettled to joke about it. I grabbed Deacon and headed to meet Brax. The three of us peered deeper into the dark, impossibly dense forest. "Could it be a trick?" I asked them both.

Illusions are certainly a possibility, Marcus said. *Many gods possess the ability to alter the surface of perception effectively. My advice is to proceed with caution in case all is not as it seems.*

"Could be." The demon shrugged his broad shoulders. "Let's go at it swinging. Whoever's on the other side will learn to regret it quick." To emphasize his point, he brandished his hammer. "I'll be the battering ram if you want."

I hesitated. "Brax, I appreciate your no-nonsense approach, but I think we should handle this a little more delicately than that. You'd chuck a bomb like a softball if you thought that would disarm it."

He frowned. "And if I was right, nobody would complain."

"It's the possibility of you being wrong that I'm worried about," I said.

He mumbled to himself and turned away. We moved forward as a group, and the shadows coalesced in front of us to fill the narrow spaces between the trees. This core of the forest stood like a fence in our way and completely blocked our progress.

"To the side," Deacon said and motioned to the left with his hand.

We attempted to work our way around, assuming the strange forest was finite, but it extended in all directions as far as my eyes could see. The other side granted us the same view.

"I'm telling you we should just go," Brax urged. "There's no point in standing around doing recon if there's nothing to see. It's obviously some fucked-up, mythical god shit, right? What else do we need to know?"

"Wait." I held up a hand to stop him. The faintest trace of a voice had caught my ear. "I hear something."

"If you say it's me bitching—" Brax began.

"No." I waved at him to stop talking. "It's people, I think." Following the voice, I moved down the path, which arced around to the right and crossed a more substantial, street-like road. From there, the voices were multiple and more distinct. I peeked from the cover of the trees. "There!"

The road we stood on led into the deepest, thickest section of this new forest, but the entrance was blocked by a patrolling contingent of guards. They didn't look particularly dangerous—at least, not more so than any standard human. But I knew from Frank and Maya that looks could be deceiving.

Brax eyed me. "Let me guess. You're not gonna let me kill them?"

"It's not because I think it's necessarily a bad idea, okay?" I said. "But we don't know what this place is, why they're here, or how many more of them there are. I don't want to run in there with our dicks out and give away our position until I have some idea of what's happening here."

"Fair enough." The demon smirked. "You don't have a dick, though."

I gave him a look. "If I did, it'd be real fucking big, and both of you know it." I pressed the button on my radio. "Luis, you there?"

"Yeah," he said. "I just did a head count. We're all good."

"Here's what'll happen." I paused and looked at Brax and Deacon for signs of last-minute objections. Receiving none, I pressed on. "We found a way into this creepy forest thing. We'll get in there, see what's up, and I'll get in touch and let you know what the next step is. Cool?"

"You're going in?" Luis sounded skeptical. "Are you sure that's, like, the best idea? This place feels…off."

"Do you want to trade places?" I asked.

"No, ma'am," he said quickly. "You go ahead. I'll wait for your signal all damn day."

"I thought so." I smiled. "In the meantime, see if you can find us more vehicles. We might need you to move fast."

"Roger that," he said. "Find vehicles, I can do. No problem."

"Thanks, Luis." I smiled. "Catch you on the flip side."

By the time I ended my exchange with the teenager, Brax had moved ahead toward the patrol post. He glanced back and beckoned me forward. He held a clump of half-dry groundcover in his hand, which he promptly lit with a swift flick of his hammer. His movement steady, he drew his hand back and launched the flaming ball off to the side of the patrolmen. In a matter of seconds, a small fire sprang up. It was quickly snuffed by ambient moisture, but the smoke it produced was thick and pungent.

The guards caught a whiff of it. They turned toward the

source of the fire and moved that way as they followed their noses and muttered to one another.

"Now!" Brax hissed. We broke into the quietest run we could manage and aimed directly for the middle of the black hole between the trees.

CHAPTER FIFTEEN

The voices of the guards faded behind us as we passed through to the interior of the strange woods. I'd expected almost total darkness, but beyond the initial border, the trees were pierced with shafts of light. We didn't have the luxury to stop until our eyes adjusted, so we pressed on through the gloom, packed tightly together and our other senses on high alert. Brax was the first to make a comment, which surprised me until I remembered he was also the one with the best low-light vision.

"Those are some trees," was all he said. Deacon and I automatically turned to look closer, and I felt goosebumps rise on my arms.

"Those are trees?" I asked out loud. Logically, I knew that was what they had to be, but the twisted, thorny formations rising from the forest floor weren't like anything I had ever seen. Their roots tangled in huge, snaking masses around the base of the trunks and spread like tentacles. The ground pitched to accommodate the place where the roots broke the soil.

"Watch your step," Deacon warned. "I have a feeling this is not a place where you want to fall."

As we passed beneath the gnarled boughs, I actually held my breath. My vision had acclimated, and now I could see the way the trees towered in uneven groups and allowed light to filter in. It wasn't a pattern I recognized from other woods I knew. The trees clumped together, then spread out, then staggered along the rutted path. I was about to wonder what might cause them to grow so randomly when I spotted evidence of a possible answer. It matched some of what we had already seen in the more normal sections of the national forest.

"Look at that," I breathed and pointed. Both Deacon and Brax's steps slowed in response. A few dozen yards before us, nestled snugly in a copse of the thorny monster trees, stood the remains of a two-story house, burnt black and moldering. Only the thickest, strongest beams were left and, really, only fractions of those. The rest of the structure lay in crumbled cinders all around its foundation.

"Somebody lived in here," Deacon whispered. A mix of awe and knowing sadness colored the words. It didn't take an ace detective to deduce what probably happened in that blackened glade.

But why? And how?

Brax shook his head. "Not somebody," he remarked. "A lot of people."

He gestured in the same direction, and I sucked in a gasp as the dilapidated shapes of civilization became clear to my eye. This house was one of many which stood at the edge of an overgrown, disintegrating curb. Heavy vines thicker than my forearm wound their way through the shattered windows of dead cars that stood where they had been abandoned in the forsaken street. A corner in the distance was marked by a rotting pole.

Deacon stopped and searched the surroundings. "I'll be damned," he murmured. "It's all around us. Where the hell are we?" He turned in a circle.

I fished out the mapping device. The signal was weak inside the dense forest's perimeter, but it managed to eke out enough to display the visual I needed. According to the screen, we stood at the edge of a whole town. The neat spread of squares, each signifying a home, store, or business, was so incongruous compared to the ravaged scene before me that I had trouble believing it was real. I dropped the GPS unit to my side and stared numbly at the ruins. "We have to find out what the fuck happened here," I said.

"I know what happened," Brax replied. As usual, he forged ahead, fearless and impatient. "It's him."

"Marcus?" I asked. "What do you think?"

The centurion sighed. *Though it pains me to make such an admission, Abraxzael's identification must be correct. There is no one else who could have this type of effect on so large an area.* He paused. *Yet it is odd to me—*

"It's weird." Brax's voice overlapped Marcus's. "I don't get what's going on here." For the first time, he stopped briefly in his tracks and gazed far down the ghost of the street. "He was never like this back in the old days."

Once again, the demon is correct, Marcus allowed. *My memories of Oxylem are inoffensive, even pleasant. He brought a spark of merriment to everyone he encountered. I believed him to be well-liked among his peers.* His tone suggested that he would have frowned if he could. *I suppose it could all have been a carefully constructed façade.*

"He had an island," Brax said in continuation of his first thought. "Before the war. I guess it was sorta like his own little utopia. As far as I know, he was happy to stay there and have beach parties with his shiny happy people, or what the fuck ever. Hell, I bet he'd have taken my sorry ass in if I asked nicely enough."

"Did you?" I raised an eyebrow.

Brax scoffed. "Of course not. They were a bunch of hedonistic drunks."

His analysis is crude, as always, said Marcus distastefully. *Oxylem and his followers emphasized a free-spirited philosophy, which included wholehearted devotion to peace. I struggle to fathom the circumstances under which his view has been altered to this degree.*

"He might be crazy," I said. "Or, at least, not himself. Noted." I trailed after Brax through the knotted trees and kept my guard up. "Does this guy have any weaknesses I should know about? Anything that'll make our lives easier if he decides he wants to trap us in here for all eternity?"

"Hm." Brax rubbed the top of his head. "Normally, I'd say fire—because of all the trees and shit, you know? But he's either already burned to a crisp somewhere, or he's made peace with that particular element, which is troubling. Fire was never his thing."

It is quite true that neither Oxylem nor his Apprenti dealt in the art of fire mastery—or anything remotely malevolent, for that matter.

"He's formed alliances," said Deacon grimly. "That's a bad sign."

"Maybe someone forced the issue," Brax suggested. "I don't think it'd be hard to convince him to do your bidding if the alternative was being cooked alive." He reached the closest side of the house's foundation and stepped across the stones. Then, he straightened and sucked in a lungful of air. "It still smells like smoke. I'm not sure if it's from this place specifically or merely in the air."

As if on cue, the wind picked up and rushed past us with a plaintive howl. It cut through the winter layers I still wore from the start of our trip, and when it died down, the howl remained.

"Shit!" Deacon shouted. "The trees are moving!"

"That's what happens when it's windy." The words stuck in my throat as I glanced around and saw exactly what he meant. On all sides, the misshapen silhouettes swayed in the aftermath of the gust. The high, keening wails enveloped us. They were the source of the haunting sound, not the wind.

Oxylem, what have you done?

Suddenly, a hand reached out and grabbed my wrist. I lashed out against it instinctively, only to see that it belonged to Deacon. "Let's move!" he shouted. "You couldn't pay me to stay here right now."

It was hard to argue, what with the freaky, screaming trees. The two of us charged after Brax, but we couldn't seem to get ahead of the noise. Every single tree in the forest had picked up the cry until my head threatened to explode. I gritted my teeth and focused all my energy on pushing forward. The shapes of tree trunks writhed in place, caught by my peripheral vision.

I suddenly stopped abruptly. I came within an inch of crashing into Brax's back. "Dude, what the hell?"

He motioned for me to shut up and nodded farther along the faint path. An eerie glow issued from the front yard of another gutted house. I took an involuntary step back.

The glow came from figures that stood in a perfect circle in earnest conversation. The one thing they all had in common was the red hair that raged against the backdrop of dusky shadows.

CHAPTER SIXTEEN

Brax glanced over his shoulder at me and held a finger to his lips. He stole forward, and his black coat skirted the ashy ground. I looked at Deacon, and we dropped into stealth mode too. The gap closed slowly and painstakingly. The more I saw of this new group, the less I liked them.

The smell hit me first—a distinctive, vaguely rotten scent that I didn't attach to the figures themselves until I saw the charred skin. They'd literally been cooked, and when they moved, I thought I saw thin tendrils of smoke curl from the peeling cracks on their bodies. Each hardened face seemed fixed in a permanent glower, even during what appeared to be a normal discussion.

The demon tucked himself behind a fallen log. I eased in beside him with Deacon. We peered over the top of the soft wood at the gathering, now less than fifty feet away. At this distance, it was easy to pick out the leader, a tall, broad brute with a stone-like slab of a face. A wiry, badly singed beard sheathed his jaw and curled over a necklace of bleached white bone. Unlike the others, his ugly mug was contorted into a braying guffaw of laughter aimed toward the ramshackle house.

"Come out, piggies!" he yelled. The tone in his voice grated on my ears, and he ejected each word with such force that flecks of spit sailed from the corners of his mouth. "The gods have arrived!" He spread his muscled arms wide and continued. "You can either emerge and submit yourselves—which, I must say, I recommend—or I'll simply burn this hovel down around your filthy little heads." The brute grabbed a large rock and hurled it at the front door, where it tore through the wood. "Don't worry. It will go quickly, like all the others. Perhaps you will suffer for three minutes, or five. But soon, it will all be over."

The next thing I heard was uncannily familiar—the heavy racking of a shotgun from inside the run-down house. The shot rang out through the hole the bearded man had made in the door, but I could tell it missed. The brute's eyes widened. His jaw dropped open in a fit of cruel hysterics. Over his laughter, a baby cried. That, too, came from inside the house.

The leader of the creepy group wiped tears of amusement from his eyes. He turned to his companions. Like him, they were burnt and reeked of flame-scoured flesh. Undisguised malice flared in their eyes. They all grinned and raised their hands. Wild spheres of fire, barely controlled, burst into being in their palms. As one, they threw the fireballs at the broken door.

This time, the screams from the house were different, now infused with fear and panic. The fire-wielders stood ready to attack. I opened my mouth to make the call.

Brax beat me to it. He charged from cover with a mighty bellow and leapt the massive log as if it were nothing more than a twig. The hammer swung from its sheath and crashed into a few of the standing bodies. They scattered before his sheer power. Instead of beating them down or snapping them in half, the demon ran directly for the threshold which was awash with licking flames.

"That crazy jackass," I said in wonder. "We have to back his ass up."

"On it." Deacon maneuvered to the best position behind the log and took pot shots at the attackers. The bullets split their cooked skin wide and exposed a coal-like layer that smoldered underneath. The wounds ejected trails of flame instead of blood, which I had to dodge on my way into the fight.

"What the hell is this shit?" I shouted as I swung my sword at the first target. "I know I've got a badass sword, but I feel like you guys are cheating!"

In lieu of an answer, something hot seared across my cheek. The skin over my cheekbone immediately blistered, and I heard the crackling impact of a fireball somewhere behind me. "Oh, yeah?" I smirked despite the pain that flared in the burn. "You think you're the only one here who can throw? Watch this!"

The *Gladius Solis* launched out of my hand javelin-style and pierced my adversary through the center of his chest. As he buckled, the blade embedded itself in an ax-brandishing woman behind him.

"Ta-da!" I said.

She stopped mid-stride, and her weapon faltered at the top of its swing. A bright glob of fire fell from her lips and seared a smoking ring into the ground. On its way back to my hand, the *Gladius Solis* cut clean through her. She hit the ashy dirt in two halves.

"Do you ever get tired of that kind of thing?" Deacon asked. He nailed two more in the head and dropped them neatly.

"Nope," I said cheerfully. "It's good for teaching these jackoffs a lesson." I held the sword one-handed, spun, and lopped off one of the intensely-red heads. Smoke and fire poured from the neck stump, and the body staggered for a moment or two. I turned my attention to the leader. "But we've done enough screwing around, haven't we? Let's take care of this problem once and for all."

He stared at me, his lips pulled back into an almost gleeful smile. "Ha!" he exclaimed and threw his head back. "It has been too long since I received a proper challenge. My only regret is that it comes from a weakling like you."

The man reached for his weapon and brought forth a two-handed hammer, its head mercilessly alight. The sight of it threw me for a loop—I'd seen one exactly like it very, very recently.

That split second of hesitation was all the bearded warrior needed. He brought that thing down with all his strength and clearly expected to finish me off in one shot. I blocked his strike narrowly with the flat of my blade. We pushed hard against each other, and our feet dug into the dirt. The cracks in his skin surged and glowed with the fire-blood that roiled beneath the surface. Drops of sweat formed and instantly vaporized off his face.

"Foolish girl," he growled as he bore down even harder. "Do you think you can alter the will of the gods?"

"No," I retorted. "I intend to crush it. And I'll…start… with you!" A war cry erupted from my throat, and I surged upward and knocked him onto his back foot. The hammer lifted as his bulky arms pinwheeled for balance. I struck out with my blade.

The redheaded behemoth was light on his feet. He hopped out of my reach and escaped with little more than a scalded abdomen. His whole face darkened into a mask of rage. I squared up and waited for his counterattack.

Instead of re-engaging, however, he simply spat at me and fled with his hammer in hand. My first instinct was to follow his cowardly ass into the woods to see if I could finish him off, but the inferno engulfed the house with Brax still in it. I turned to face the roaring heat.

It was suffocating, overwhelming. I had a tough time even inching toward the flames.

Victoria, do not! Marcus exclaimed. *My feud with Abraxzael notwithstanding, you could not survive that environment on your own.*

The last of the roof caved in and sent a plume of flame higher still. I shielded my eyes as best I could from the unrelenting force of the fire and squinted toward where I'd seen the demon disappear. The door was all but gone, engulfed in a writhing maw of flame.

Suddenly, the outline of a man burst through that impenetrable wall of heat. Brax leapt onto the cool, cinder-dusted dirt, his arms full. His coat had been wrapped around two bundles held tightly against his chest, and a third clung to his back.

Deacon and I dashed forward as soon as he landed. The first bundle was the baby we'd heard before the fire started.

Smears of soot stained her cherubic cheeks, but she gripped the edge of the coat with the unmistakable vigor of the living. The moment her little lungs drew in the fresh air, she burst into tears once again.

The young woman who had fallen from Brax's back stumbled to her feet and reached for the child. Her pretty face was dirty and stained with tears. "My babies," she sobbed, and the words hitched.

CHAPTER SEVENTEEN

Brax lifted his coat to reveal a second child. The little boy seized his mother's skirts and howled almost as loud as the baby. The whole forest shook with the siblings' cries until their mother pulled herself together enough to sing a snippet of a lullaby. She gathered her son onto her lap, cradled the infant in the crook of her arm, and rocked them while she crooned softly. Both children gradually calmed. I knelt at the young woman's side.

"Are you all right?" I asked and kept my voice as gentle as possible. She had a shell-shocked look in her eyes. "Is anyone hurt?"

She stopped humming the melody and turned her gaze to me. "No, I don't think so." She ran her hands over her children and checked them for injuries. "Not hurt." She shook her head. "But we're freezing and hungry. And we're alone." She drew a shaky breath. "I fear everyone else is dead."

Rather than voice my agreement, I laid a hand on her

arm and tried my hardest to channel Jules. "What's your name, hon?"

"Laurel," she said shakily. "It's Laurel. And these are my little ones." She brushed her fingers tenderly over the boy's hair. He turned shyly toward me. His eyes were the same clear blue as his mom's.

"Hi, Laurel. I'm Vic." I smiled. "My friends and I will take you to a safe place. Can you tell us anything about where we are right now? Is this where you're from?"

"It was…" Laurel trailed off. She sniffled through a new wave of tears. "I wanted to raise my family here and build a life. This was our dream house." Her thin shoulders slumped. "But something happened to the forest a while back. The trees…they came alive. And they were angry." She gazed with numb fear into the depths of the surrounding wood. "I don't doubt they still are."

I exchanged glances with Deacon and Brax. "They're angry," I repeated. "Tell me about that."

The poor young woman shuddered. "They can move, but I don't know how. All that really matters is that they do it. Jesse says he saw it happen once or twice. Always at night, he says. When no one's looking. Isn't that right, Jesse?" The little boy nodded, his eyes wide and solemn. His mother continued. The sentences tumbled as if released from behind a great weight. "I used to love watching him play in the field. We took walks and went bird watching and looked for bugs." She chuckled hollowly. "There aren't any birds now. I don't even know if there are bugs."

"But there's something," Deacon prompted. He took his

jacket off and draped it around her shoulders. "Here, take this. You three are nothing but skin and bones."

"We couldn't leave," Laurel told us. She talked barely above a haunted whisper. "I waited too long to try to get us out, and by the time I knew we didn't have a choice, the place was full of those horrible burned ones." She ran her palms vigorously up and down her arms. "We've laid low for days, even after we ran out of food. The water is low too. I don't know what to do."

"Hey." I shifted so that she could see me clearly. "I told you, we'll take you out of here, and I meant it, okay?"

Laurel chewed her pale lips. "It won't be easy," she said. Her hand tightened on my sleeve with a surprisingly strong grip. "We made a run for it once, but we had to come back." Tears brimmed above her lower eyelashes. "Can you imagine? I had to bring my babies back to this awful prison."

I squeezed her arm. "That must be how they finally found you," I said. "I'm glad we got here in time."

She shook her head. A specter of fear drifted across her face and settled deep into her half-starved features. "Something else is waiting deeper in the forest." Her volume dwindled down to almost nothing. "A monster."

I examined her closely to discern whether this information was paranoia-fueled fiction or actual fact. She looked at me with bare, frightened honesty, and I decided to take her words at face value—for now.

I offered her my hand, and we both stood. "Let's get you safe," I said.

She lit up with hope. "Thank you. Oh, thank you so much. You're an angel."

Deacon and Brax moved in around her and her son. After a peek at the GPS, I directed us back the way we'd come, and we began to walk.

We weren't alone for long.

Loud, boisterous voices drifted through the trees, capped by the braying laugh of their bearded leader. Laurel froze like a deer in headlights. Instinctively, she searched for a place to hide. "Don't run off," I cautioned her and held her arm. "We'll defend you. Trust me. We are your best chance."

She cowered and trembled visibly. Her little boy tugged at her skirt. "Mommy?" he asked loudly. "Are the bad guys back?"

Laurel shushed him, but it was too late. The voices fell dead silent the moment the child spoke. They picked up again and grew louder as they angled directly toward us. Deacon, Brax, and I stepped together to form a living barrier between Laurel's little family and the barbarians who shortly materialized from the uneven tree line.

The leader emerged first and planted his feet in a wide, immovable stance directly in front of me. His grin had become more of a snarl, and as he bared his teeth, more of his forces appeared to surround our party. There were too many for us to handle without backup. His troops filled the spaces between the trees as far back as I was able to see.

"Going somewhere?" the leader demanded with a leer. "It's rude of guests to cut and run, don't you think?"

Brax clenched his fists. "Get the hell out of our way."

"Or what?" The brute ran his fingers through the red coils of his beard. "You'll fight like a fool and be killed where you stand? That's fine by me."

Laurel screamed in horror as her kid bolted from the safety of her embrace. His huge eyes were crazed with fear.

The warrior strode forward and reached one burly arm past me with lightning speed. I lunged to deflect him, but he was deceptively quick.

"No!" Laurel sobbed.

"See this rat?" he asked and lifted the little boy by the ragged collar of his shirt. "Make one wrong move—one tiny move that I don't like—and I'll burn him alive. The other one, too." For emphasis, he pointed at Laurel's face.

She flinched, her gaze locked on her son as tears streamed down her cheeks. "Please don't," she pleaded. "Please!"

"Hear that?" asked the leader. He snorted. "The lady doesn't want me to cook her little piglets." He scowled. "I didn't think so. Does anyone have any objections?"

I glanced at Deacon and Brax. The agent knew an impasse when he saw one, but Brax? I wasn't so sure. The blatant, white-hot rage scrawled across his face didn't offer much assurance that this wouldn't end in copious amounts of bloodshed. I tried to get him to make eye contact with me so I could signal him with my eyes, but everything except the sneering redhead had ceased to exist in his world.

One second ticked by. It might as well have been an hour. The kid, still held aloft, had begun to cry again, though he did not squirm. Brax's black eyes flicked to the boy's face.

Finally, he stepped back. His rage had obviously not cooled, but he chose to stand down for maybe the first time in his life. Following his lead, I put my hands up at shoulder height, palms out. Deacon did the same.

The brute laughed. "So, you have some sense after all. I'm surprised—but not yet impressed. There will be time for that later." He tucked the kid under his arm. "This, I keep. Call it insurance."

Laurel sobbed. I wanted to comfort her, but I didn't dare turn my back on the leader.

"March, piggies," he commanded. "A new destiny awaits."

CHAPTER EIGHTEEN

The redheaded barbarians herded us deeper into the twisted trees, their weapons at the ready. They watched us like hawks for any suspicious movement. Behind me, Laurel cried quietly and clutched her baby to her chest.

I could feel Brax smolder with barely contained fury, though I didn't dare look in any direction except forward. We marched in silent formation along the overgrown track. The soldiers' footsteps were a steady drumbeat in my ear. Under the leader's burly arm, Laurel's son hadn't moved a muscle.

The path deteriorated significantly at the end of what had formerly been the town's main street. Gnarled root balls marred the way, some as wide around as my waist. Hardly any grass grew in this place. Mostly, only debris littered the ground. My foot kicked a ragged plastic bag half-buried in the mud. The skeleton of a shopping cart lay on its side, its wheels long gone. More houses appeared, each looking at least as run-down as Laurel's.

A tableau of destruction, Marcus said.

I kept my mouth shut, followed in the leader's wake, and did my best to project a docile image. I had no doubt that we'd be slaughtered if they caught even the slightest whiff of resistance—most likely starting with Laurel's closely guarded son.

The tribe had shepherded us a quarter mile before the sound of other people pierced the quiet. Coarse voices conversed in a language I didn't understand over more and more footsteps. We turned a bend, and I saw a pack of the same redheaded warriors who led their own captives. I looked into the frightened eyes of dozens like Laurel. Some of them were in even worse shape.

Our leader stopped, moved back, and motioned for us to join the new throng of prisoners. Acting against every ounce of logic in my brain, I did as he indicated. Deacon and Brax fell into place next. They did their best to shield Laurel from the newcomers' prying eyes. She kept her head down, but she couldn't resist shooting fearful glances after the leader as he strode toward the front with her child. Her trembling fingers dug into the baby's thin blanket.

I managed to get near enough to grab her free hand and squeeze it. She froze, but the ghost of a tiny, grateful smile settled on her lips. Providing her a shred of comfort made me feel slightly better, and I didn't release her hand as we resumed our march. Most of the enforcers were out of my line of sight, but I knew they were there and flanked us like sharks that had penned in a school of prey.

The walk went on forever, and the farther we went, the harder it was to take it quietly, despite Laurel's hand still shaking in mine. She had finally stopped weeping, but her eyes stared blankly ahead. I turned to Deacon on my other side and whispered, "Can you look after her? I want to see if I can work the crowd a little."

"I was thinking the same thing," Deacon replied. "Probably better you than me." We changed places, and his fingers brushed the small of my back. "Good luck."

I slipped through the crush of bodies and looked for anyone who could potentially be coaxed out of their shell. Hardly anyone noticed as I passed, and when they did, it was only for a second. My attempts to start conversation were met with little more than tight-lipped stares. The atmosphere was heavy, cold, and fearful. I pushed it away. The single thought present in my mind was that I needed to get *something* started there—if not a full-scale revolution, then at least some civil discontent.

But everyone was either terrified, demoralized, on their last legs, or a combination of all three. One of the guys I approached was so short of breath he couldn't even respond, and his friends shooed me away. Plus, I had to be wary of possible eyes on me at all times and of the fact that the soldiers might see my purposeful movement as a threat. I darted a few feet at a time and tucked myself as close to the absolute center as possible. The longer I could stay out of sight, the better.

In all honesty, I really didn't have a real plan. I merely didn't want anyone to get in my way. For once, all I wanted to do—all I *could* do—was talk.

I lost track of time fairly quickly as I weaved through that living maze. At least a dozen more interactions fizzled and died in the cold. A young woman finally stopped me as I cut carefully in front of her. "You're wasting your time," she told me, and her lips barely moved. "And you're putting us all in danger. We've accepted the inevitable. You should too." She directed her dark eyes to the ground at her feet.

"You can't all think that way," I said. "I'm trying to help." The situation was dire; I understood that. But the air of insurmountable hopelessness crept under my skin. I refused to subscribe to that way of thinking. My own tribe had been through worse. Finding a way, however, required a will, which was sorely lacking at the moment.

Victoria, I have ruminated over our new acquaintances. Perhaps I can be of some assistance.

"Go for it." I wound slowly back toward Deacon, Brax, and Laurel, a little glum and relieved to hear a helpful voice that wasn't my own. "There isn't much else at the moment."

It remains puzzling to me that these particular Forgotten should have teamed up with the likes of Oxylem, but they do remind me of one individual in particular. His name was Hyrrik. You might have considered him similar to human Vikings.

"Known for their hospitality," I quipped. "I guess that explains all the burning. And now we can safely assume there was pillaging, too. That would have kept me up at night for sure."

I detect trace amounts of sarcasm in your tone, he said flatly.

I brushed it off. "I'm more interested in why the hell this dude and Brax use the same hammer. Maybe not exactly the same, but you know what I mean. It can't be a coincidence."

For that, you will have to ask Abraxzael yourself. In which case, you are on your own. He sounded a little sullen. *I refuse to engage with him.*

"Suit yourself," I said. Marcus fell silent, and I approached the demon's dark, brooding figure. He didn't acknowledge me as I fell into step beside him. I wanted to roll my eyes a second time, but I restrained myself. "Can I ask you something?"

"You will regardless," Brax said. "So why not?"

I sighed. "Geez, don't cut yourself on that edge, my man. All I want to know is, what's the deal with your heroic first-responder routine back there? For someone who never shuts up about how little he cares for humanity, you sure came dangerously close to giving a shit."

The demon gritted his teeth and obviously regretted the fact that he hadn't ignored me outright. He said nothing for at least thirty seconds. "The baby's cry reminded me of something."

"Okay," I prompted and angled for more. "Of what?"

That time, he stonewalled me completely. His hands were shoved deep in the pockets of his coat, and his face was unreadable behind those black glasses. A palpable barricade had gone up in front of that line of questioning. I reversed and tried a different tack.

"I saw you talking to Jules before we left. Did she give you a locket or a valentine or something?" It was meant to be a joke, but he didn't take the bait. His expression remained inscrutable.

Before I could say anything else, a shout rang out. Everyone flinched collectively. "Separate!" the warriors at the front shouted, their weapons raised. "Women and children to the left. You pathetic, weakling men, to the right. Now!"

The formerly grave-silent herd of prisoners erupted in a wave of emotion as we realized we would be separated. In the instant it took to look at Brax, he had already been drawn away. Deacon squeezed my arm as he moved past.

I bolted for the burly leader.

He saw me coming. "What now, you pesky wench?" he demanded. "You're starting to annoy me."

"Where are they going?" I asked. "Why are you dividing us?"

"See for yourself," he said and swept his arm out. In doing so, he dropped Laurel's son. I gathered the child up quickly, prepared to stand my ground. But now that we'd blended into a larger populace, the brutish man didn't seem to care that much about the boy. He glared and shrugged. "Look."

The path ended ahead, and the claustrophobic ranks of trees gave way to a surprisingly wide and open clearing. Massive, sawed-off stumps dotted the dead plain. Once I comprehended what I saw, my heart sank. This was the true national forest, or what remained of its ruins. An army of emaciated men labored to cut down the trees that were left. Thick, rough-looking vines chained them together, and when one collapsed, the others in his gang all stumbled.

"What the fuck?" I whirled to look for Deacon and managed to catch one last glimpse as he gazed back at me. In a split second, he was gone in the rush of other men, and I was prodded forward.

"Enough questions," the leader said brusquely. "Let's

go." He led us toward where the trees were still the thickest around the edge of the clear-cutting. The trunks felt more like the bars of a cage now between us and that horrific scene.

I wasn't sure which side I wanted to be on.

CHAPTER NINETEEN

If nothing else, I was able to reunite Laurel with her son and released the boy into his mother's open arms. She wept with joy although she didn't dare stop walking. He clung to her skirt. I took her hand again.

"Thank you," she said through tears. "Thank you so much. I thought…" She couldn't bring herself to finish the sentence.

"Don't worry," I reassured her. "It'll be okay."

Skepticism furrowed her brow. "I'm not sure." Her voice dropped. "There are monsters in these woods. We've never been out this far, and with good reason." She talked softly as if she were afraid the others would hear. "I wasn't kidding when I said we never left the house."

The mention of monsters had roused the little boy's interest. He peered out from behind Laurel with wide, bright eyes but she shook her head and didn't elaborate.

I wracked my brain for a way to extract more information without acting like a jerk. She was clearly traumatized, and she was not the only one. Every woman I saw had that same haunted expression. The last thing I wanted was to make it worse, but I also needed to understand all possible threats.

Laurel didn't volunteer anything more after that, and I didn't want to leave her side. I remained silent and mulled things over in search of the best angle of approach. My thoughts were interrupted by a familiar moaning howl from the trees.

"Slow!" came the call from the front line. Our movement ratcheted down until we barely shuffled forward, which struck me as a little odd. I stretched to peer over the group at the redheaded soldiers. They were on full alert and their wide eyes peered into every dark nook and cranny they could possibly see. I frowned. Were they looking for something? Wary of an ambush?

Suddenly, they didn't act like the top of the food chain, and that concerned me.

Something tugged at my jeans, timid but insistent. I glanced into the round, sweet face of Laurel's son. "Can I tell you something?" Jesse asked somberly.

I bent to hear him better and slipped my arm around his shoulders. He nestled up to me, and even though I'd never been what some might call a kid person, I felt my heart melt a little. "You sure can," I said, my tone light. "What's up?"

"Do you hear that?" He pointed vaguely to indicate the ethereal noise that resounded through the air. "That's what the trees say when they know he's coming."

The ominous way he spoke sent a chill through my blood. "Who's 'he?'" I asked.

The kid's giant blue eyes panned the surroundings.

From his vantage point, there was little to see other than legs and feet. "The white wolf," he proclaimed reverently.

I bit my tongue to keep from spewing my instinctual response, which was along the lines of, "And who the hell is that?" It turned out not to matter anyway. Before I had the chance to utter another word, a different howl eclipsed the first. This cry was louder than the trees as if it came from even greater multitudes. And it was all around us.

"Stop!" the leader bellowed. "The enemy approaches. Do not back down." At once, all his subordinates drew into a tighter circle, tense and ready. I strained to see what they watched for, but inside, I already knew. I'd worked side by side with one for too long not to recognize the battle cry of a Were.

Their first strike was swift, merciless, and immediately overwhelming. The wolves surged upon the flame-haired Vikings like a tidal wave of terror and ripped into their ranks. The women screamed, but it was drowned out by the cacophony of soldiers dying in droves. In a matter of seconds, flames flickered as they bled from the Vikings' wounds.

"Oh, hell no," I said and went quickly into full evacuation mode. "Listen to me!" I shouted above the din. "We have to get the fuck out of here if we want to live. Follow me!" I grabbed Laurel by the hand yet again and her kid too.

She beckoned to the woman beside her. "You can trust this lady," she said. "She saved my family."

The woman looked at her, then at me, and nodded with grim determination. "If she can help us through this," she said, "that's all that matters."

"Stick together!" I called. "But move fast. The fire will spread."

Smoke already hung in the air, tinged with the acrid scent of burning hair. The screams of the dying followed us as I herded the flock of women and children away from the fight. Some of them covered their ears, and most of the kids wailed, but many of the mothers stood strong and resolute. They were tough. They'd seen a lot of shit.

I stopped in a place with clean air, far enough from the bloodbath that we'd have ample warning if the fire got out of hand. "Stay here," I told the group. "We won't move unless we're in danger."

"What's happening?" Laurel's boy asked me. "Are there more bad guys now?"

"Could be," I said. I was grateful for the werewolves' intervention—to a point. They weren't all like Maya, but they could all wreak havoc like her. "I don't know for sure, so we have to be careful, all right? Stick close to your mom. Keep her safe."

He nodded gravely. Laurel scooped him into her embrace. I drew my sword and threaded through the trees toward the massacre but not too far from my group. The worst mistake would be to leave them defenseless. I glanced over my shoulder once to give them some sort of assurance, and at that moment, the best I could think of was a thumbs-up. They did not look very comforted.

"Nice one, Vic," I said under my breath. "Now they probably think you're a lunatic too."

Lunatics can still have honor, said Marcus helpfully.

I sighed. "Thanks, buddy."

The clash grew louder in my ears, and so did the

crackle of the building inferno. Tongues of flame danced amid the trees, which were splashed with wolf blood and ashes. Through the thickening smoke, I caught an eerie silhouette of a Viking soldier torn to shreds by one of the beasts. A figure emerged from the melee and barreled toward me, wild-eyed. His beard was half burned off his face, but I recognized the Viking leader. His air of cockiness had been replaced with one of crazed fury and bitter desperation.

"You!" he shouted and fixed his blazing eyes on me. "You must have lured them here. You must have known."

"Known what?" I asked. "That werewolves are insane and also super strong? Yeah, I'm not an idiot."

He bellowed an anguished roar. "Shut up! Shut up!" The head of his hammer swung high and lit a corona in the surrounding smoke. "I'll torch you." His voice was hoarse, and his chest heaved. "That will fix it. I'll end it all and wipe the slate clean. Gods forgive me—"

The last sentence was mangled by a grunt of pain as a huge, dark shape bore down on him from the side and crushed his body into the ground. The former Viking leader groaned and twisted futilely under the force of a great, grizzled paw. The creature that loomed over him was enormous, vicious, and covered in white fur. It was missing an eye and a foreleg. In place of the limb was a long silver blade.

The wolf turned to me and exhaled a furious breath. I stared into its face and asked, "Smitty?"

I'd never seen a Were smile before, but the old guy managed somehow. "Vic," he said. "I thought you'd never return."

CHAPTER TWENTY

"Well, I'll be damned." I grinned. "Good to see you, Pops. Any chance you can get us the hell out of here?"

Smitty winked. "Sure I can. But I gotta warn you. It's gonna get worse before it gets better." His Were voice was deep and gravelly, a fitting match for the grizzled silver wolf who towered over us. Two other Weres appeared to take responsibility for the captive Viking. "No time to waste." Behind him, the bloody battle climbed toward a crescendo. "Come this way. Don't fall behind, now."

With that, he led us to the right so we could circumvent the worst of the fight. I ushered the women in front of me in order to make sure no one was left behind. Smitty moved fast at the head of his new pack. He cleared debris out of the way with broad sweeps of his arm and his gleaming silver blade.

"It's okay," I said to the group. "Believe it or not, I know this guy. He's a friend—and the best thing that could've happened at the moment."

Nobody seemed totally comfortable, but no one argued either. Given the alternative, Smitty the friendly werewolf was quite obviously the lesser of two evils. As our band of escapees picked up the pace, I made my way back to the front and Smitty's side.

"Where are we headed?" I asked. "Because we're missing some people, and I really don't want to screw off and let them fend for themselves."

Smitty glanced at me. "I have my men already on it," he said. "Trust me. They'll be fine." A grimace of disgust crossed his lupine features. "These warmonger jackasses don't stand a chance."

Heartened by his response, I let myself relax a little. "I'm glad to know you still have your community together," I told him. "Maya will be happy to hear that, too."

He smiled fondly at the mention of the vet's name. "I wondered if that girl had come back with you," he said. "It's a pity she didn't. There are a lot of folks who would've liked to see her back at HQ."

"Sorry," I said sheepishly. "She wanted to be here, but the fort couldn't spare both of us. Someone needs to hold it down, right?"

He chuckled coarsely. "You have yourself a fort?"

I nodded. "An old military base in the middle of bumfuck nowhere. It's a pretty sweet setup, but I needed someone there I could trust while I'm gone."

"Makes sense. Tell me what you're doing way out there in the wilderness. You were pretty set on getting back to your city last time I saw you."

"I was," I said. "And we did. We stayed for as long as we could, but the gods eventually ran us out. It turns out New

York is a coveted battleground in this war, and I decided I'd rather save lives than hold my ground."

Smitty nodded approvingly. "That's a sign of wisdom," he intoned. "We heard snippets along those lines from the girl on the radio. At least until all hell broke loose about a month ago." He grinned again and bared his impressive fangs. "She and Amber were about tickled pink when they found out they both knew you. I guess it ain't that surprising if you think about it." His gaze made a quick circuit of the woods around our troop. "I'll tell you more when we get settled. I can't afford to get too distracted while we're out here. Just because there's a fight on doesn't mean we're safe."

I craned my neck to look toward the canopy. The howling from the trees had faded somewhat as we relocated, but I could still hear it in the distance. The ones in our immediate vicinity hummed although they weren't as loud or insistent. "Do you know what's going on with this forest?" I asked. "I've never heard anything like it. A little bird told me it happens a lot when you're around."

"Yeah," Smitty said. "They do that whenever any wolf is nearby, really. At first, I thought it was a fear thing like they assumed we would attack them. I saw it like the members of a herd protecting each other, alerting everyone to the presence of predators." He brushed his claws lightly against a trunk. "Now I kinda think it's a different story. They're more like cheerleaders in their own way. And they scare the shit out of those damn matchstick men, so I don't complain."

I gave him a sidelong look. "You're talking like these trees have feelings, you old hippie," I joked.

He shrugged his grizzled shoulders. "Well, they might still. They were people once."

I can confirm that the werewolf is correct. The trees in this section of the forest are souls that have been converted by Oxylem. Traditionally, this process occurred by their choice, but I am quite sure this has not been the case for some time as far as the vast majority is concerned.

I drew in a sharp breath. Suddenly, the disfigured trees seemed to stand out in much greater detail and commanded more of my attention. "These were all—"

Smitty put a finger to his lips. "When we get to where we're going, I'll fill in all the gaps," he said in hushed tones. "For now, I'd like us to move a little quieter. We're close, and I don't want to be tracked."

I shut my mouth, but thoughts raced in my head. It had not occurred to me that the creepy forest itself might be made up of its former inhabitants. The revelation that we had essentially walked through a living graveyard sent a shiver up my spine. I glanced back toward the battle we'd left. The prospect of a forest fire loomed even grimmer than before.

Smitty dropped until he was almost on all fours. At a distance, he could've passed for something like a real wolf. He was still too bulky, too shaggy, and too purely wild in face and shape, but he had clearly learned a hell of a lot about surviving in his current form.

I sidled as close to his furry side as I could get. "How far?" I breathed inches from his ear. He lifted one arm and pointed into an outwardly impenetrable wall of under-brush. I hesitated and glanced back at the women and chil-dren who trailed behind us.

He moved ahead, dove into the foliage, and opened a path down the middle as if it were water. Quickly, I motioned for the others to follow close behind and went in after him. We stayed low and waded through a scratchy sea of dead leaves and branches. The tunnel narrowed briefly before it widened into a more normal path.

At that point, Smitty straightened. He loped toward the edge of a bright, warm clearing. "That's our home base there," he said. The words were tinged with pride. "We worked hard to build ourselves up after that epidemic."

I smiled, happy for his success and eager to be among friendly faces. "I can't wait to see it."

He stepped through the tree line. "You don't have to wait, 'cause here we are." We paused to take it in. "Welcome to the resistance, Vic."

CHAPTER TWENTY-ONE

"Wow," I murmured.

The clearing, like every other location we'd seen so far, was massively overgrown and returned slowly to its natural state. Twisted tendrils of roots pushed their way through the soil as far as I could see, despite the fact that few trees grew beyond the point where we stood. In the center of the space, a huge stone structure soared into the sky.

The empty frame of a former window gazed down on us like a blinded eye to tell me that this place had once been a church. Time and the elements meshed its austere glory with the ethereal beauty of the wild. Vines twined over mossy stone, holes crumbled in the façade, and trees pushed through the eroded floor and reached for the roof. But its walls held firm, and the doors at the top of the sweeping entrance stairs were fortified with iron.

"A stunner, isn't she?" Smitty remarked. "Someone smiled upon us when we found her more or less intact." He wasted no time and herded our troop of escapees into the building, including me.

The towering doors creaked open, and a warm wash of light poured over our weary group. Smitty's people waited across the threshold to welcome us with open arms. Some of the women burst into tears in the face of such hospitality. Others were joyfully reunited with the brothers, husbands, and sons who had made it here ahead of us.

"Damn," I said to Smitty. "You weren't kidding about having that covered." I turned to pat him on the shoulder, but the wolf had gone. "Where the hell did he go?"

"Hey, stranger." The grin that popped onto my face as soon as I saw Deacon was automatic, born of sheer relief. He pulled me into his arms for a quick squeeze. "Check these digs out." He left his arm around my shoulders.

"You think they're nicer than ours?" I asked. The church wasn't as big as Fort Victory, but its sanctuary was nice and open and allowed enough room for beds and other things. Dozens of people milled around to settle the new arrivals. The smell of a hot meal in the making wafted down a hallway.

"Nah," Deacon said. "But there's more of a rustic charm."

"I wouldn't call this place rustic," Brax interjected. He had appeared out of thin air, as was his wont, and as usual, he seemed thoroughly unimpressed. "Overbearing, maybe. There are a bunch of creepy statues near the front."

I gave him the once-over. "I'm surprised you're not literally on fire, Brax," I said.

He folded his arms. "That's a new one. Tell it again, why don't you?"

I chuckled, released Deacon, and scanned the room once more for Smitty. He walked toward us, a wiry old blacksmith with a full white beard. The sword in his arm socket bore a sheath, and he smiled with his entire wrinkled face. Everyone he passed greeted him like an old friend—in many cases, he probably was.

He guided us toward the far wall of the sanctuary, where a closed door led to the church's inner office. "Gentlemen," he said and nodded to Deacon and Brax. "How are we doing? All in one piece?"

"Yes, sir," Deacon replied. "Let me take this opportunity to thank you for saving our asses. You showed up in the nick of time."

Smitty laughed. "We've had practice, my boy. Maybe too much of it." His expression sobered. "And it didn't start here. The fighting's been on and off since you left Washington all that time ago, Vic."

He parked himself in a metal folding chair and fished a pipe from the front pocket of his overalls. "The wolf disease spread farther than we thought it would," he said. "More of 'em cropped up in droves—overnight, it seemed. Our original clan did the best we could to track them down and try to talk it through."

As he spoke, he pinched tobacco from a pouch and used his thumb to tamp it down into the bowl. "It was easier after Lupres was dead. All that mind control trash from before went out the window." Smitty frowned. "But then again, that made it harder in some respects too." He delved into his pocket for a match, which he struck on the sheath of his arm-sword. "Not everyone saw the same safety in numbers that we did. Many times, I was told to screw off, and they left to make their own way.

"Too many turned against us, and we had to wage our own civil war. I can't tell you how much blood was shed in the early days, but it was a damn river. Lord knows I didn't want to do it. I don't think anyone did." He paused to take a puff of the pipe. The blue smoke plumed from his lips. "Still, we knew we had to do it, so it got done." He sighed and shook his head. "Of course, we buried them all. You go back there, and you'll find a veritable cemetery. What a shame." Another puff released a billow of sweet-smelling smoke. "The silver lining is that there was a surprising number who did come with me. That's how we got here."

"You have an awesome operation," I said. "I'm impressed."

He looked at me. "Things didn't take off until the gods came back. First, it was that jackass with the hammer bigger than his head. Up until then, we got by however we could and lived off our wits and the good graces of the outdoors. We could turn and hunt or turn and stay warm if we needed to, so we figured we didn't need to be tied to a base. We planned to head east to see if we could join a bigger piece of civilization."

"Why didn't you?" I asked.

"We heard New York fell, and it wasn't long before that god came sniffing around to claim his piece of the pie. He looked like an extra in one of those hero movies and called himself Hyrrik. He and his soldiers swarmed the land like a plague, and they brought fire wherever they went. You saw the evidence."

"We did," I said and thought of the scorched forest on

the way in. "It looked like someone had burned towns for fun."

"That's about the long and short of it," Smitty agreed. "They rounded up all the residents first, though. Anyone who resisted was either restrained or cut down. Everything that couldn't be stolen was burned." He adjusted the stem of the pipe between his teeth. "The big boss is gone now, and we've done all we can to resist and to collect former prisoners. But it's hard to make real progress when we don't have the numbers to press the advantages we get."

"Simple," I said and patted the *Gladius Solis.* "Step one, we find this fucker. He can't hide forever. Step two, I get in as close as I can. Step three, I end him."

To me, the blueprint for our attack was clear. But to my chagrin, old Smitty shook his head. "If it were that simple," he said, "we would've done it already. When I say the boss is gone, I mean he's dead because the first thing I did was lead a team in with the express intention to kill him. The fight was grueling. We lost many great people. But in the end, we got the bastard." Smitty chuckled wryly. "The rest of them didn't like that too much."

"I salute your courage and your success," Brax spoke up abruptly. He looked directly at Smitty. "Hyrrik was no weak fool. I know because he was the one who enslaved me the first time. He gave me a taste for violence and blood. And when I left, I took his hammer with me." A smirk tilted the corner of the demon's lips. "My only regret is that the beast is already dead—I would've enjoyed that sweet retribution myself."

Nobody really knew how to respond to that. I could

feel Marcus radiating incorporeal disapproval. Deacon broke the silence by asking Smitty, "Then what?"

Smitty puffed on his pipe. "Well, another god dropped by. A young one, nice looking, but he had a whole slew of monsters like I'd never seen that followed him around. It looked like the forest had come to life almost. But there was something wrong about it all." The blacksmith leaned back in his chair. "We thought maybe he might be peaceful, or at least nonconfrontational, but no such luck. The rest of the fire guys defaulted to this kid's command, and he simply picked up where the first left off. And let me tell you, they were hopping mad about us having the gall to challenge one of their own. The very first thing they did was purge a huge number of our forces as retribution. Hundreds, maybe thousands. That was when we ran into the forest and finally set up here."

I had to keep my jaw from falling open at the end of his story. The gods I had known had been violent and greedy to an extreme, but I had never encountered this kind of wholesale destruction up close. An immediate wave of guilt surged through me. If I'd known that thousands of people struggled to survive on the west coast, I might have come sooner. "Damn it to fucking hell," I muttered.

"That young guy and his monsters are the ones who make the trees like this," Smitty continued. "Don't quote me, but I think every time they kill someone, one of those trees pops up real quick like. They grow like the dickens, too. My guys think they're haunted. Bad juju, as they say." He shrugged one shoulder. "I'll be honest. It caught me by surprise. If you saw this god, you'd know what I mean. He doesn't look the type."

"I have seen this behavior from the gods countless times," Brax said, his voice sour. "The acts of cruelty aren't without purpose. Most gods will rule through fear if given the choice. They find it to be the most effective tactic—they make themselves into great symbols of terror."

Abraxzael is correct about this, but I am not sure I believe that Oxylem would have gone this way. His character never harbored such deep darkness.

"It makes sense," Smitty acknowledged. "But those trees are more than symbolic. They harvest them. You would've been too if you'd gone where they wanted you to go."

The image of the lumber chain-gang flashed through my mind. "That clearing," I said. "Oxylem is chopping down his own trees."

"Bingo." Smitty pointed a finger at me. "They razed the old ones first, mind you. I think there's something about these trees that he needs or that *somebody* needs. The men who get captured work until they drop dead. Then a tree sprouts where they fall and a new body comes to do the chopping."

"What's the wood for?" Deacon wondered. He had an expression of morbid curiosity on his face like he already understood the answer would be something he didn't actually want to know.

"Hell if I know," Smitty replied. "We can't risk going back in to find out because I'm not sure we'd survive another round of retribution killings. We have to preserve what we've got. But the rumor mill's churned for a while about how this tree god and the fire guy are small potatoes compared to whoever they're working for."

"I wonder who that is," I mused.

"No clue about that either," the old man said. "But I betcha I know someone who does." A keen spark lit in his eyes as he pushed himself from the chair. The pipe, still full of the dregs of his smoke, disappeared into the pocket. "Come here. I wanna show you something."

The four of us walked toward the back of the church into a cold, lonely room tucked away behind the altar at the head of the sanctuary. Its only feature was a heavy boulder in the middle of the floor. A broad-shouldered, beefy male had been chained to the huge rock. His fiery hair fell in ragged clumps over his face. When he saw me, he snarled.

CHAPTER TWENTY-TWO

I smiled sweetly at the Viking leader. "You can't get enough of me, can you?" I asked.

The man growled like a rabid dog, and he almost foamed at the mouth, too. He looked out of his mind with rage and humiliation.

"I'll handle this." Brax stepped beside me and cracked each knuckle with quiet deliberation. "You two might want to step outside for a while."

Deacon and I looked at each other. "Right," the agent said. "Consider us gone."

We left as the demon advanced on his helpless prey. The door had barely closed behind us before we heard the first screams.

Smitty coughed. "If you young people will excuse me, I have business to attend to." He winked. "A revolutionary's work is never done."

"See you later, Smitty," I said. "Thanks again."

He smiled at me. "After what you did for us, this is the

least I could do for you." He ambled off to another part of the church, his blade arm swinging casually by his side.

I sat down against the wall and leaned my head back on the cold stone. Now that things had calmed down for more than five minutes and we were safe, exhaustion settled deep into my bones. I closed my eyes. Deacon sat beside me as another high-pitched screech emanated from the other side of the door. It was accompanied by an unfamiliar sound that I eventually identified as Brax's laughter. "At least one of them is having a good time," I remarked.

Deacon chuckled. "This is not exactly the venue I had in mind for our first date," he said.

I gave him a look. "We're on a date? And did you just say 'venue?'"

He shrugged. "They teach you some five-dollar words at the academy." He scooted a little closer and put his arm around me. "It's not exactly a date, but considering the days we've had, I feel like it's about as close as we'll get for now." More laughter leaked through the wall, accompanied by a sizzling sound. "The experience might be enhanced by some noise-canceling headphones, though."

"Note to self," I said. "Next supply run, raid an electronics store."

Deacon added, "And find a plug that works or some good batteries. It'd be nice to have some other electronics again."

"What would we use them for? My cell phone's been dead forever, anyway, and it's not like there's much data service left. We might be able to find pockets if we're lucky, but unless we went to California where Namiko is, I wouldn't count on it. There are so many nerds out there that they have to have something rigged up."

He squeezed my shoulder. "I like how you give them enormous amounts of credit and call them nerds in the same sentence."

"Nerd isn't a bad word." I rest my head back against the wall. "And that's what they are. I'm nothing if not honest."

"Yeah." Deacon stretched his long legs. "I always admired that about you, even when we weren't necessarily on the same side. You might have made me as mad as hell, but there was never any bullshit." He thought about it. "I mean, not really. You did tie me to a bed that one time. That wasn't too far from here, actually."

I glanced at him. "You talk about it so much, I almost think you enjoyed it."

"Well, maybe, if things had ended differently," he answered. "Did I ever tell you that the maid who found me called the entire housekeeping crew? She said it was because she didn't know what to do, but I think it was so they could all laugh together. I had to bribe them not to call the police."

I snorted. "Did you tell them you *were* the police?"

"Hell, no. I would never have heard the end of it. As it is, I barely escaped with my life."

I shrugged. "I think you're a little dramatic, but I'm sorry, nonetheless. I merely tried to help you build charac-ter. And keep you out of my way."

"Look how that worked out for you," Deacon replied.

I patted his leg. "Don't be so hard on yourself. You're getting better. At least now, you know who's in charge."

We both grinned at that, and a warm, companionable

silence filled the space between us. Every breath made his chest rise and fall behind my shoulder, and I felt my eyelids grow heavier. I thought he had dozed off too, but his voice roused me out of a pleasant half-sleep. The soundtrack of Brax's little interrogation session formed a morbid lullaby.

"Hey, Vic."

I opened my eyes. Deacon looked at me, our faces inches apart. "What's up?" I asked. "Don't tell me you want to bust in there and stop him. Something tells me the demon from Hell wouldn't appreciate that, and I won't act as anyone's human shield."

"No, no." Deacon smirked. "I wanted to say, about that kiss earlier—"

He was cut off by another shriek and an accompanying bout of gleeful belly laughs from Brax. I placed my hand on his chest and slowly but firmly pushed him away. "Sorry, Romeo. American Psycho in there is kind of killing the mood."

The FBI agent shook his head. "Damn girl," he said. "Remind me never to take you out to a horror movie."

I frowned. "Hey, man. If I have to pay ten bucks to see a movie, you better believe I'll watch that shit."

"Let's say I pay," Deacon countered. "Hypothetically."

That made me smile. "Then we can talk."

Neither of us wanted to interrupt Brax's session with the Viking leader. The demon took his time, and Deacon and I took comfort in not having to do anything except listen to the information being extracted.

"This is kind of nice," Deacon remarked. "Except for all the screaming."

I ran my fingers through my hair. "I only hope the guy

doesn't die before we can talk to him. Brax is okay, but I can see him getting carried away quickly. I think there's some bad blood there. Did you see how quickly he charged into the fire?"

"Let's be real," he said. "With Brax, there's probably bad blood everywhere."

I glanced down at my medallion. "No kidding."

A few more minutes passed until the howling finally died down. Seconds later, Brax yanked the door open. He stepped into the hall, his coat smoking and his face and arms covered in burns.

"Holy hell," Deacon said.

I raised an eyebrow. "How's it going?"

The demon grinned more widely than I'd ever seen. His wounds didn't seem to have any effect on him at all. He beamed at us. "Jerry is ready to talk now," he said.

CHAPTER TWENTY-THREE

I almost choked on air. "Who?"

Deacon stood first and pulled me to my feet. We stared at the demon.

"*Jerry?*" I asked.

Brax stepped aside and gestured to the open door. The Viking leader slumped against the rock in his chains, surrounded by little pools of fire. Whatever damage had been done to Brax, Jerry had clearly received the brunt of the punishment as evidenced by the cuts and bruises all over his body. He had his head down, and his chin almost scraped his chest. His beard had been burned down to patchy, charred stubble.

"Doesn't he look like a Jerry?" Brax asked.

He looked like he'd been hit by a truck, although I couldn't feel too much sympathy for the man who would have killed us all. He'd earned this and more.

Even though Jerry the Viking was in a bad way, I stepped cautiously around him in case he still had some tricks up his sleeve. He didn't look at me until I got close and then he squinted through the eye that wasn't swollen shut. A trail of blood trickled from his lower lip.

"Hi, Jerry," I said.

He sighed so deeply, I thought his lungs were turning inside out. "You win," he rasped. "I tapped out. I wish my men were half as brutal as this piece of shit."

"Thank you," said Brax, with no small amount of pride. "Now talk, or I'll get back to work."

Jerry turned his bloodshot eye to me. "What do you want to know?" he asked. A bit grudgingly, he added, "Anything. No secrets."

I stood in front of him. "First of all, thank you for your cooperation. And for giving Brax something to do for the last forty minutes. We're not always fighting, see, and he gets bored." I moved closer to the disgraced Viking and knelt to stare into his face. "Let's start at the beginning. Tell me about yourself and how the hell you got caught up in this mess."

He seemed surprised, but he didn't deny my request. "Okay." Jerry coughed harshly and sucked in a breath. "Look, I thought I was a pretty bad dude back before all this started. Me and my boys ran with a rough crowd, and we were proud of the bullshit we got up to. Breaking and entering, vandalism, car theft. A couple of armed robberies, a lot of beatdowns on the streets. Real tough guy shit." He grimaced. "It was a good life for us. We had a lot of fun. Fuck the police, fuck the rules, fuck bitches. You know." He fidgeted, and the chains jangled. "I guess I always knew I was really on the bottom of the totem pole. There were guys who had stockpiles of money, weapons, fast cars, all that stuff. They could have snapped their fingers and gotten me killed in half a second if I ever stepped out of line. But I never thought about it that much until Hyrrik showed up."

"What happened then?" I said.

Jerry glared at me. "He told me I was weak. He said I wouldn't amount to anything unless I got off my ass and seized power from those who kept it for themselves. At first, I was pissed and thought 'who the fuck does this scumbag think he is?' But I realized he was right, and I started to have ambitions. I wanted to be the big dog for once, to have people follow my lead instead of the other way around. Hyrrik gave me the power to make it happen." He paused. "The only thing was, he had a catch. If I didn't do everything he said from that moment on, he'd take everything away." He shrugged. "So what? He made it sound like he and I wanted to do all the same stuff anyway, so I agreed. It wasn't so bad. Much like the way it had been, but better."

"And then?" I asked.

"Then he died. I guess I ought to thank those fleabags for killing him because the weeks after that were the best of my life. We ruled this place exactly the way we wanted to. For a while, it was like the old times went into over-drive. Nobody told us what to do, and if they tried, we torched 'em. Total freedom." He actually looked wistful as he spoke. "But it didn't last. The vamps showed up not too long after Hyrrik bit the dust. Since then, we've been under their thumb."

"The vamps?" Deacon interrupted. "I thought you were working for Oxylem."

Jerry brayed with laughter at the mention of the tree

god's name. "Please. That guy's a candy-ass. He was so grateful to be rid of Hyrrik that he didn't dare stand up to us, but the vamps rounded him up just the same. They made him turn his followers into trees, and then they made him sic them on everything else. He cried the whole time, the puny wimp. There was nothing else he could do."

Brax looked slightly puzzled. "He's a god," he said. "He should have at least put up a fight."

"He's a peace-loving hippie, is what he is," Jerry spat contemptuously. "He didn't have a chance against the vampires. These guys would've torn him to shreds if he so much as thought about saying no."

Deacon glanced at Brax and me. "I don't get it. I thought the vamps were all scattered now. There's no one left for them to follow."

"Don't look at me," the demon muttered gruffly. "I've never understood those slimy fucks."

"You don't know much, do you?" asked Jerry. "The vamps have always had a leader, and what's more, they fuckin' worship him. I mean, they treat this dude like the god to end all gods. I heard them talk about him, and Oxylem's worked his punk ass overtime to get things ready. Supposedly, he's gonna come calling any day now. That's what all this destruction is for."

"A show of power," I said.

"That's it." Jerry nodded. "The vamps want to show him they're worth their salt, or maybe they don't have a choice. He doesn't sound like the most charitable guy in the world. They make it sound like if he goes to the trouble of showing up and doesn't like what he sees, he'll wipe us all out."

"That's great, but who are we talking about here?" I'd started to pace without even noticing, but my eyes remained fixed on Jerry. "I hope he has a name, for your sake."

Off to the side, Brax cracked his knuckles again.

Jerry flicked his eyes to the demon and back to me. "He has a lot of names," he said nervously. "It depends on who you ask. Some of the vamps call him the Angel of Death, which is pretty played out if you ask me. Some of 'em call him the Serpent of the Shadows. Some simply call him the Quiet Man."

"I'll need something a little more specific," I told him.

Brax moved to the knuckles of his other hand.

Jerry swallowed. "I heard Oxylem say it once," he ventured. "He whispered it like even the name scared the shit out of him." He paused as if he, too, was reluctant to release the name into the world.

"Out with it, Jerry," I said tersely. "Trust me when I say you can't afford to dick us around."

The Viking's jaw clenched. Brax closed in, and he flinched visibly. "Delano!" he shouted. "The name was Delano."

CHAPTER TWENTY-FOUR

"Wait, what?" I lifted my hand to the medallion around my neck and squeezed it to signal Marcus to tune back in. "You're sure that's what he said?"

"I swear on my right hand," Jerry confirmed. "Delano isn't the most common name in the world. Nothing else it could've been."

The man speaks with conviction, Marcus chimed in. *I do not perceive him to be lying, although I do find his information troubling.*

That didn't make much sense to me. In the few encounters I'd had with Lorcan's favorite Apprenti, he never seemed like the biggest threat in the room. Sure, he was important to his boss, but I always figured he was more of a glorified errand boy, a fancy secretary with weird shadow powers. A yes-man above all else. The idea that he had enough power to terrify another god or to keep an entire region in line didn't fit with the version of him that I knew.

I voiced my skepticism. "I don't know, dude. I've had

run-ins with Delano before, and he wasn't *that* great. Besides, I'm the one who killed his boss. If he was super strong, why didn't he come kick my shit in right away?"

"Beats me," Jerry said, genuinely bewildered. "From what I've heard, he sounds like a damn psychopath. Maybe he couldn't care less who you killed. Or maybe it made his life better like it did for me."

I kicked at the floor. "Shit. What do you think, Brax?"

The demon studied Jerry's downturned face. "Unfortunately, I'm inclined to believe this rat," he said. "There's an old legend about Delano from way back in the old days. About how he managed to become an Apprenti."

You must understand, Victoria, that the Apprenti are not like a god's other followers. The deal must be struck by both god and intended Apprenti, and the process typically requires great sacrifice on both sides. It is not something any god would do without a reason, least of all a deity as selfish as Lorcan.

"I'm listening," I said.

"You don't need me to tell you what a royal asshole Lorcan was," said Brax. "He was around for a long time, and yet, no Apprenti. My guess is that he was a picky son of a bitch who couldn't find a flunky to lick his boots clean enough. That, or he didn't want to give anything up for the sake of someone he'd undoubtedly view as a slave. Whatever the case, he was on his own for ages until Delano finally came along. The legend is that Delano was human at some point. He had his own little kingdom in a corner of the world and everything. Came from an ancient line of rulers. The people thought the sun shone out of his ass."

"Sounds like he had it made," I said.

Brax nodded. "That's the thing—you'd think he did. I'm

sure those poor serfs gave him everything he ever demanded. But once he became Apprenti to Lorcan, the whole kingdom went up in smoke. His palace, his gigantic family, every single thing that had ever been his was gone." Brax snapped his fingers. "Like that. Not a trace left behind."

"I don't get it," I said. "Wouldn't that make him hate Lorcan's guts? Why would he work for the douchebag who murdered his family?"

The demon looked at me like I was an idiot teenager. "Read between the lines, Vic. Lorcan didn't kill Delano's family. He did it himself as a fucked-up tribute to Lorcan. He made them an offering to prove the strength of his loyalty."

I paced faster as my mind spun to make sense of what I had heard. A strange, acrid scent leaked into my nostrils, but I ignored it under the weight of my thoughts. Would Delano have done something that heinous merely to secure a spot at the right hand of a god? Suddenly, I remembered the way he had looked at me whenever we were face to face and the way his pale eyes could pierce to my core. And I knew that yes, he would.

Abraxzael's rendering of the legend is crude but accurate, Marcus said. *There is no reason to believe that those events did not occur as described. Delano may have seemed utterly subservient while Lorcan was alive, but his meek exterior is only a façade. He is as cold-blooded and ruthless as they come, and he would stop at nothing to secure his nefarious aspirations. If what Jerry says is true, if Delano has found a way to gain real power, there is no telling what he could do with it.*

"We have to stop him," I said. I lifted my head, and the

weird smell from a few minutes ago struck me full force. I furrowed my brow. "What the fuck is that?"

Behind me, Jerry laughed. It was a wild, uneven sound, hampered slightly by his injuries and the smoke that now poured into the room from a line of roaring flames. One of the Viking's larger wounds had begun to bleed a steady stream of fire, which we'd been too distracted to notice. Now, the room filled slowly with an inferno.

Brax lunged forward as Jerry's chains snapped from heat and stress and the Viking managed to strike him square in the jaw. The demon stumbled backward from the unexpected force and out of the circle of fire.

"You morons!" Jerry jeered. "You thought you won because you got me to spill my guts about Delano, but the joke's on you. It doesn't matter what you know if you're too dead to tell anyone else. Soon, this place will be nothing more than a pile of bones and ashes."

"Damn it, Jerry!" I yelled. "This is how you repay us for letting you live?"

He didn't reply at all except for more hoarse guffaws. The flames whirled in an orange curtain. I drew my sword and channeled all my frustration into forward momentum.

On the other side of the wall of fire, I could hardly see anything. Thick smoke stung my eyes and tried to push its way into my lungs. Using the outline of the boulder as my guide, I pressed forward until Jerry was right in front of me. He stood upright, no longer shackled.

"I'll admit you're braver than I thought you'd be," he said. "But it doesn't matter. You're too late."

"Fuck you," I said as I raised the blade and ran it through his chest. "How about that?"

The Viking died without another word.

Before his body hit the floor, I slammed the *Gladius Solis* down at my feet and conjured a shield around me. The flames that licked at my skin were shoved back by the golden shell of protection. I knelt in front of the sword and concentrated on widening its range. Gradually, the fire receded. It consumed most of Jerry's corpse with a voracious hunger, and finally, short on fuel, it began to fizzle out. I didn't move a muscle until I was certain that a threat no longer existed. Only then did I allow the shield to come down.

Deacon and Brax moved forward as soon as I stood. "Are you okay?" I asked Brax. "He slugged you pretty good."

The demon scowled. "It's nothing. What about you? I haven't seen too many fireproof humans."

I glanced at my arms and the backs of my hands. All the hair had been singed off, and the surface was pink and blistered. It stung, but I was no stranger to pain, and I could already sense the nectar working in my blood.

"I'm fine," I said. "And Jerry's dead as shit. But most importantly, the church won't burn down."

Brax grumbled. "You never let me kill anyone important."

I patted his shoulder. "Sorry, buddy. Maybe next time."

CHAPTER TWENTY-FIVE

A ruckus outside drew our attention away from the dying embers of Jerry's last stand. Old Smitty burst into the back room, wild-eyed, and brandished his augmented arm.

"What the hell is going on back here?" He flung his other arm across his nose and mouth as the smoke hit him and he coughed into the crook of his elbow. "I thought you were going to interrogate him, not burn him at the stake."

"He's the one who did the burning," I replied. "Don't worry, Pops. We've got it under control. Our subject got a little well done in the process, though." I gestured to the body on the floor.

"Good riddance," Smitty said. "Did you get anything useful out of him beforehand?"

"Yeah," I said. "He thought it'd be safe to tell us everything since we would all die after the interrogation was over. He told us that Delano is the brains behind this whole operation. Kind of a mistake on his part, but we're not complaining."

Smitty waved us out of the room and backed out himself before he uncovered his face. "Let's get on out of that barbecue pit before these old lungs up and quit. I'm not as young as the rest of you whippersnappers."

"Weren't you smoking a pipe earlier?" Deacon asked innocently.

The blacksmith rounded on the agent and narrowed his eye. He might have only had one eye, but that didn't lessen the intensity of his gaze. "You," he announced, "have graduated from whippersnapper to rapscallion. You better watch your step, young man, unless you want your ears boxed."

Deacon hid a smile. "Sorry, sir. I merely made an observation."

Smitty held his glare for a few seconds longer. Then he grinned and slapped Deacon on the back. "I'm fooling with you, boy. The pipe's a bad habit, don't I know it. But if you can believe it, I've felt damned good since I started on the old hair of the dog, so to speak."

Deacon blinked., "Hair of the—oh. Right, of course, that would make you more...durable."

We followed Smitty back into the church's main sanctuary, which was enveloped by warmth, lively conversation, and the smell of a home-cooked meal. He paused near a large bin full of an assortment of clothing.

"Yeah," he said and looked into the bin's contents. "A lot of us were pretty peeved about it in the beginning, but that all changed once we realized how much more ass we could kick. Now, I think we're all settled into our identities. We keep these crates of clothes out to make the transformation process a little, uh, smoother."

"Got tired of flashing your junk to the world?" I asked.

"Something like that." He picked through the items and found a shirt with a long rip in the middle. "Mind you, sometimes, this type of thing happens, so we gotta keep an eye on what ends up in here or else it'll be only a bunch of filthy rags." He shot me a smile. "I bet you didn't think there'd be that much laundry in the resistance, but it keeps the gears moving."

"Hey, that's an awesome idea," I said. "We should do that at the fort for Maya. She's always trying to figure out a way to quick-change without showing off the goods."

"It's worked out well for us," Smitty said. "I wasn't sure how any of this would go at the start, to be honest with you. But so far, we've managed to grow our community despite the odds. And I gotta tell you, we have a mind to keep fighting no matter what."

"That's good to hear," I told him. "We're in the same boat."

The old man gave me a sidelong look. "Sounds like there's a 'but' on the way."

"Well…" I scratched my head. "It's apparently indisputable that Delano's the mastermind here. I wish I knew more about what the hell he thinks he's doing. I never was able to get a motive out of him in New York. I don't think I realized he had one, which makes me feel incredibly stupid now."

"Delano?" Thoughtfully, Smitty rubbed his whiskers. "That the name you said earlier? I've heard it before."

"Really?" I tried not to get excited. "Where?"

"The girl on the radio mentioned it a few times. Now if only I could remember *her* name."

"Namiko?" I volunteered.

He snapped his fingers. "That's it! Very nice young lady, and smart as a whip. She and Amber got along like two peas in a pod." His expression darkened. "She told Amber this Delano fellow has popped up all over the world and caused destruction everywhere he goes. He always leaves a pile of bodies in his wake—humans and gods alike."

"Bastard," I muttered. "Has she been able to get a bead on him at all? I know she's stuck manning her hub in California, but we might be able to track him down if she has any leads."

Smitty shook his head. "Amber said it's not so simple. There are rumors about him everywhere, but none of the stories match up. She's heard a million different descriptions of him doing a million different things. The only real consistency seems to be the name."

"What the hell does that mean?" Deacon asked.

I gritted my teeth. "It means we've found our new priority number one. And you guys know what that means."

"New plan?" Deacon asked knowingly.

I smiled at him. "New plan."

We spent the next few hours at the drawing board with Smitty and some of his top strategists to hash out the next steps that, for the first time, didn't really involve me. The reasons were solid once I understood, but I still went to bed feeling more than a little bummed. Not only that, but I quickly discovered how spoiled I'd been by all the creature comforts at Fort Victory. There was something incredibly humbling about a shower taken with cold water, a sponge, a bucket, and a thin sliver of soap.

"Marcus?" I asked when I lay in bed with the medallion on my chest. "Are you awake?"

Always. What is on your mind?

"What do you think Delano's up to out there?" I asked. "Maybe it was naïve of me, but I didn't think I'd hear that name after we defeated Lorcan. I'm not sure what to expect."

In all honesty, neither am I, Marcus said. *A part of me hardly believed the legend might be true, and yet, he appears to have pulled the wool over many, many eyes.*

"And now he's killing gods," I said and rolled onto my side. "That's *my* thing. This dude's seriously cramping my style."

It is surprising to me that his power should have increased to this level within such a relatively short space of time, Marcus said. *This may be a sign of other forces at work. You will have to stay vigilant, as always. Keep your eyes open and your chin up.*

"Sure," I agreed. "It'll give me something to do while I twiddle my thumbs from the sidelines."

I tossed and turned for a long time after my conversation with Marcus drifted into silence. My room in the church was a private one but cold, and as I lay cocooned in the blankets, I did my best to think ahead to the future and where we were going and what our next moves might be. But despite my best efforts, my thoughts constantly returned to one thing above all else.

Tomorrow, Deacon would ship out on the next mission —without me.

I didn't get much sleep that night, and I woke in the sourest funk. I still got ready quickly so I could at least be there to watch the guys roll out. We had decided that too many would make them conspicuous, so Deacon and a small group were the only ones who prepped to actually leave that morning. The plan necessitated that every one of them be men, since women wouldn't be allowed on the lumber gangs.

That meant I had to sit this one out completely. It wasn't the only reason, but it was the one I liked best. I reminded myself of it over and over on my way toward the church's exit. The front of the sanctuary buzzed with activity and excitement. Smitty's men were hyped at the prospect of getting to face another big battle. I'd done my best to warn them that if they saw Delano, he'd be nothing like Hyrrik, no matter how strong the fire god had been. I told them to be careful, to be smart, and not to jump the gun. All of this was stuff they already knew, obviously. We were a band of veterans by now, and Smitty's Weres didn't really need my advice.

I was worried that they didn't understand what they were in for. What if Delano saw through our scheme and didn't take the bait? What if he countered with a preemptive strike? These were good men—great men—and yet, Delano's wrath was apparently mighty as hell. I wished more than anything that I could go with them. That was what I thought about when Deacon found me with a sullen scowl plastered on my face as I stood near the wall.

"Don't look so happy to see me," he teased gently. "You didn't have to get up so early. We'll be fine." I looked at him and felt like the tables had turned on me. He was the cocky, confident one who threw out quips and grins at the crack of dawn. My mind raced with worry, my hands knotted deep in my pockets. "Seriously, Vic. We'll be okay."

"I want to go," I told him and hated how petulant it sounded. Part of being a good leader was knowing where I had to be, and for this mission, my place was to stand guard at the church. Unfortunately, the facts of the matter didn't make it sting any less.

"You can't," he said bluntly, although his tone wasn't unkind. "Remember all the stuff we talked about? If we want to draw this mofo out from whatever rock he's hiding under, then you have no choice but to lay low for now. That sword is awesome, but it might as well be a damn beacon straight to your location. He might be able to use it to bypass us directly and come straight to you. That's bad."

"It is," I admitted. I had trounced Lorcan way back when, but everything I heard made it sound like Delano's power had long since eclipsed that of his former boss. The odds of a one-on-one match weren't reliably in my favor. I was not the only god-killer on the block, which still made me a little salty.

"Plus," Deacon continued, "we know nothing about Oxylem's state of mind, other than Jerry's opinion. I'll go out on a limb and say he wasn't the greatest source of intel. But if Oxylem is as big a wimp as Jerry claimed, he might crack as soon as he hears you're around. The whole thing is ruined if Delano bails because he's afraid of you punching his face in."

I frowned. "Yeah." As pissed as I was, it was somehow reassuring to hear that Deacon had such a solid grasp on the things we'd discussed at our last-minute meeting. He had come a long way since his induction by fire into the world of the gods. I was proud of him, and I told myself to lighten up.

"Don't forget, Vic." He put his hands on my shoulders. "This is your plan, and it's a good one. We'll infiltrate the lumber crew ranks and grow the rebellion from the inside. From there, we can see what state these people are actually in, what our prospects look like, and how many we can recruit. We dig in, expand as much as we can, and wait so we can be ready when he finally shows his ugly mug. Then we dive in and take him and Oxylem out in one fell swoop. Free the slaves, save the world, and come home safe and sound. That's the point."

"I know, I know." I ran my fingers through my hair. "It'll be dangerous." For some dumb reason, the words, "I'm worried about you," stuck in my throat and wouldn't come out my mouth.

Deacon smiled. He knew what I tried to say. "None of it's as treacherous as hanging out with you. I promise."

I couldn't help a low chuckle. "Touché."

He reached down and grabbed my hand. "I'll make you a deal. You be careful here, and I'll be careful there, and when I get back, I'll cash in on that rain check I took."

I laughed a little more. A blush crept automatically toward my cheeks. "You're on, St. Clare. I'll have you know I take my deals very seriously."

Deacon winked. "So do I." He glanced around at the men who assembled near the door. "It looks like we're about ready to go. See you soon." He gave my hand a quick, warm squeeze, and I watched his back blend in with the rest of the group all clad in torn, dirty clothes. They had made every effort to hide their vitality from the Vikings who would shortly capture them and turn them loose in the prison camp with the others. I could still tell they were strong and healthy, but I knew to look past the surface.

My chest felt tight as I watched them march out together. I followed across the threshold and onto the top landing of the stairs. The group spread out as they hit the yard so as to not look too much like the guerilla detachment they were. Deacon's dark, tight curls stood out to my watchful eye. I wanted to run after them.

I didn't. Common sense and my sense of duty formed a loud, insistent chorus in the logical sector of my brain. This was no time for emotions. They had this. I had a million other things I could do. For instance, I had yet to update Luis and the others on our current situation. They'd heard that we were holed up with Smitty in an old stone church but not much more than that. Another example of my stellar leading skills.

I turned somewhat guiltily to enter the church and fetch my radio from the bedside table in my room. Luis's company had stood by for almost two days. It was high time to get in touch again.

Chin up, Victoria! Marcus said cheerfully. *Your role is no less vital on the home front.*

"Thanks, man. I'm good." I took a deep breath and shook the tension from my shoulders. "But it sucks not being on the front lines. That's all. I wanna see the action."

Truly the noblest of desires. Fear not! Your hunger for battle shall not go unsated if I know anything about Delano and his ilk.

"Good," I said. "I'm dying to see him again." I took a step toward the door, only to be halted in my tracks by a young, spunky female voice.

"What in the hell are you doing here? And why didn't anyone tell me?"

The tone of voice, though playful, immediately got my hackles up. I was not in the mood to be sassed by anyone. I turned, and the flat annoyance on my face was replaced by a grin I couldn't possibly suppress. "Amber!"

Her smile lit up her whole face. "Long time, no see, captain," she said.

CHAPTER TWENTY-SEVEN

We stared at each other for a minute and grinned like loons until she finally motioned for me to go inside. "Please," she said. "Don't let me slow you down. That's my way of saying it's as cold as balls out here and I'd rather not freeze my ass all the way off."

I laughed and retreated into the sanctuary. Amber stepped in behind me and blew into her gloved hands. Her cheeks were rosy, and her eyes sparkled as brightly as ever.

In the few minutes of silence that followed, I studied her. She was tall and sinewy, and even her face seemed chiseled. This girl was clearly as tough as freaking nails. But even that kickass aura did nothing to dim the sunny smile that radiated from her features. The first thing she did was grab me in a huge bear hug.

I gasped as the wind was knocked out of my lungs. "Shit, you're strong."

"Hey, thanks." The girl beamed brighter yet. "As it turns out, weeks of cruising the woods will make you into a pretty formidable beast." She pulled back to inspect me in turn. "It's so good to see you. You have no idea how excited I was the first time I heard Namiko say your name."

"Aw, shucks." My mood had lifted a thousand notches in the few minutes I'd been blessed by Amber's company. "Where the heck have you been, anyway? I've bummed around this place for the last couple of days and I haven't seen hide nor hair of you."

"That's because I have a job now," Amber announced proudly. "I'm the lead scout. Eyes of the camp. It means that more often than not, I run around outside and look for important stuff, collect whatever intel happens to float around, call the Weres to the places where they're needed, and snipe for them if I can." She quirked an eyebrow. "That last one's my favorite. Are you surprised?"

I shook my head, impressed. She was barely breaking out of her sheltered shell when I left Washington to return to New York. In a matter of months, she'd blossomed into a completely rad, badass flower.

"That's one hell of a dangerous job," I said, suddenly the adult in the room. Uncool of me? Maybe a little, but I couldn't help it. The girl wasn't even twenty years old.

Her grandfather was the one to come to her rescue. He strode up behind her and said, "My granddaughter's become a rather dangerous person." He smiled. "And we're all better for it."

"Good for you, old timer," I said and gave him a thumbs-up. "It's nice to see you loosen the reins."

"Tell me about it," Amber said. "He drove me nuts."

Smitty shrugged. "She had to grow up fast, and I had to choose whether to protect her or let her survive. I chose the latter. And along the way, I've come to understand that a little danger can be good for the soul."

"I've told you that for *years,* Pops," Amber said and nudged him in the ribs.

He winked. "Stubborn as a mule, your granddad is."

I groaned. "A little danger sure would be good for my soul right about now."

"I wondered why you were standing outside, but I didn't want to come right out and ask," Amber admitted. "It seemed like it might be a touchy subject."

I folded my arms. "Oh, it is. But it's mostly me being dramatic, I guess. I have to lay low so those guys can go undercover and do things all stealthily. I hope they pull it off, really. But it means I have to take one for the team and park my ass on the bleachers." I pursed my lips. "Which I hate. A lot. They've been gone less than ten minutes, and I can already feel myself going stir crazy."

Amber eyed me, puzzled. "Wait, why do you have to lay low? I've seen you do tons of stealthy shit before. You sneaked all the way into the wolf lair."

I chewed the inside of my cheek. "It's a guys-only field trip," I explained. "The easiest thing to do was to get in through the lumber gangs, and those are only men." I patted the sword on my waist ruefully. "That, and I have this thing. I'm a freaking lighthouse to the gods right now."

"That's lame," said Amber, with the infinite wisdom of youth. "It doesn't make much sense to me, either. We have plenty of women out there fighting every day and night. And you especially would be so valuable."

"Sword," I reminded her and pointed dramatically.

She stared at me. "Just don't use it, Vic. That's what you

said is the real tell, right? If you don't whip it out all over the place, you should be good to go."

I held in my shock at her suggestion. Partially because it seemed so simple once she'd said it out loud, and partly because not using the sword struck me as similar to not using one of my limbs. The *Gladius Solis* hadn't been out of my reach since I'd gotten it from Marcus, except for one ill-advised decision to leave it in the general's safekeeping. "I mean…" I finally managed to say something. "I guess that's true."

Under any other circumstances, I might be 'freaking out,' as you are wont to say, said Marcus. *I must confess, the idea of going into battle with the sword restricted still causes me anxiety. However, I also understand your need to be in the middle of things, and as I implied before, it is a need I must respect.*

"It's the blade that identifies you, isn't it? I would think you could move undetected as long as it's not lit up." She glanced at her granddad. "But if you're not sure, you can always leave it here. Pops will take good care of it."

"On my honor." Smitty saluted. "You've seen how tight we run this ship, Vic. We're not about to spring a leak now."

"I trust you." I unfastened the sheath from my belt and hefted it in my hand before I passed it to him. My heart palpitated a little, but the feeling of bare panic faded quickly and was replaced by a sensation of general nakedness. My belt hadn't felt that light in a long time. "I think it will be nice to go incognito for a while."

"That's the spirit," Amber cheered. "Man, you're so cool. I can't wait to bring you out there."

I had to grin again. Her enthusiasm was infectious. "Where are we going?"

"Oh, you'll love this." She gave Smitty a kiss on the cheek and waved as we retraced our steps out the door. I almost paused and thought of Brax, who'd also been exiled from the lumber gang mission. Then I realized that if I was recognizable, he was a neon billboard on a moonless night. Merely the sight of one of the Marked would tell any discerning Forgotten that something was hinky. I kept my mouth shut and Amber went on. "I got word about an hour ago that there's a supply caravan moving through the forest. Naturally, I tracked it down, spent a while charting its course, and then I called my people in. They're waiting for us as we speak, so we'd better hightail it. We're gonna rob this thing like it's a steam train in the Old West."

I cracked up. "You're ridiculous, Amber. I missed you."

"Didn't you?" She shot me one more huge smile before she headed toward the edge of the forest, fearless in the face of the encroaching gloom. I followed gladly. The welcome rush of adrenaline pounded through my veins.

I was so happy to be back on the hunt.

CHAPTER TWENTY-EIGHT

We ran for a long time before Amber showed any signs of slowing. She wasn't a Were, but damn, the girl had stamina for days. She was like a laser beam homed in on her target location, which was a stretch of rugged forest path she clearly knew by heart. On the approach, she signaled for me to cut left as she went right and melted seamlessly into the trees. I found a good hiding spot, hunkered down, and waited for company.

The loss of their leader had not made Jerry's soldiers more discreet. They ran up with all the grace of a herd of water buffalo and crashed single file through the woods. Most of their weapons were lit and poised to defend and threw flickering tongues of light ahead of them. I peered out from behind the cover of a giant, sturdy log and noticed that the fire Vikings weren't alone. Humans were sprinkled in their midst and towering, bark-covered tree Goliaths trudged alongside. The human soldiers looked beaten down, hungry, and thin. They wouldn't pose much of a threat.

Amber crept up to my position while I scanned the incoming train. "Looks good," she whispered. "Everything's going to plan so far. When we go in, focus on the Vikings and the trees, okay? The regular people won't be a problem. They're all half-starved as it is."

Her analysis and target selection were spot-on. A tidal wave of pride swelled in my heart. "Right on," I said. "Will everyone else come from the same side as us, or are there allies across the track? I want to know what to expect."

Amber pointed up and down the thick underbrush lining our edge of the narrow passage. "We're all over here. The idea is to overwhelm them in numbers, and either stamp them out or chase them away. I'd feel better if they were dead, but as long as we get what we came for, it doesn't much matter what happens to them."

Another more excited whisper cut into our conversation. "Amber! It's Jayna. Am I late?" The question was followed by a slim figure which dropped into place on my other side. She looked at me with huge golden-brown eyes. "Oh shit, sorry. You're not Amber."

Amber suppressed a snort of laughter. "I'm right here, Jayna. That's Vic, and she's super cool. She'll help us with the operation." To me, she said, "Vic, this is Jayna. She's newish, but she has a ton of potential."

"I can't wait," Jayna whispered. She was hidden like us, but every fiber of her being practically vibrated with anticipation. "This is my first big attack. It'll be terrifying. And so much fun!"

I bit my tongue. This kid couldn't have been more than in her late teens, and the roundness of her face made that seem like a stretch. Her bouncy demeanor was totally at odds with the task at hand, but that was what she'd shown up to do, and if she had qualms about it, I couldn't tell.

Jayna quieted and settling into a calmer, more intent state as the convoy drew level with us and began to rumble by. I listened for Amber's cue.

It didn't come until the last crate-loaded cart was past our hiding spot. She pulled a radio, pressed the button, and said, "Go time."

An ear-splitting explosion rocked the woods. Up ahead, a whole mess of dynamited trees cascaded into the convoy's path. The carts bumped to a halt amid a hail of colorful curses. The human soldiers swiveled in a panic and searched for the ambush they knew would come. In these parts, attacks were rarely random.

Amber leveled her trusty rifle and pulled the trigger. A swarm of Weres had already poured in from the tree line to choke the convoy and its guard. Jayna leapt from my side with a shrill howl.

I fought every instinct and stayed beside Amber, taking potshots with my own gun. My bullets made way less of an impact than hers. I was fairly sure I could count the real hits on one hand. It wasn't a great feeling, but I pushed through it, determined to do my best. The shots continued to go wide, ricochet wildly, or occasionally, find a target in an enemy.

"I miss my sword," I muttered, but I made a mental note to suck up my pride and maybe ask Deacon for some shooting lessons later. He'd almost certainly make fun of me, but at least I'd know how to handle myself in the future and not waste ammunition.

It was fucking hard to hit moving targets.

I fired much slower than Amber too, and in the lull between my reports, a high, fearful yelp cut through the chaos. I snapped my head in that direction and caught a glimpse of the young Were Jayna squared off with one of the mammoth trees. The monster's branches were hooked at the ends and razor sharp. They'd make total mincemeat of a werewolf's flesh.

"Fuck, cover me!" I shouted to Amber.

"I got you!" she answered instantly. No questions.

I waited for an opportune moment to make my break through the furious melee, and when it came, I lunged out of cover and raced across the frosted ground. A couple of fire Vikings dove toward me. I flattened as low to the ground as I could, and they crunched together at full force directly above my head. One of their flaming weapons seared a patch of skin on my shoulder and burned through my jacket before it clattered to the ground. Both the smell and the pain were completely ignored. All I saw at the end of my vision was the tree bearing down on Jayna, its branches poised for violence. She coiled to spring in its shadow, but it was easy to tell she didn't have enough time to launch herself.

Not without help, anyway.

Less than thirty feet away from her, my view was suddenly blocked by another Viking soldier who attacked with a glowing mace. I ducked, and a bullet zinged over my burnt shoulder and buried itself right between his eyes. He dropped like a meaty sack of bricks. I vaulted over his body. The tips of the tree's vicious branches came within inches of Jayna's bristled fur.

"Jayna!" I hollered and slammed into the side of the

tree. I hit it so hard that fiery shocks of pain rocketed through my arms and I clenched my jaw against them. "Get out of the way!"

I clawed my way up the trunk. The branches swung wildly and scrabbled to slice at me instead. The rest of my jacket tore free from my torso. It landed on top of one of the carts.

Jayna's eyes went wide. "Vic!" she barked and sprang from her coiled stance to lash at our shared adversary.

Her mass and our combined strength rocked the tree backward and forced its branches to spread into a stabilizing formation. The beast staggered.

"Get the bark!" Jayna yelled. "It's like armor. Get the bark!" She ripped at it furiously, and the tree screamed. Its branches pinwheeled in a desperate attempt to pry us off before she could inflict permanent damage.

Around us, the Vikings raised a cry. The leaders of the caravan lifted their weapons and shook them so the flames danced. Righteous anger burned in their eye, alongside the promise of vengeance. But the Weres refused to be deterred, and Jerry's comrades were forced to retreat.

The tree-beasts lumbered with them in great, long strides through the woods. Jayna released the lattice of deep scars she'd made, and we stood together to make sure no one turned around. Bodies—mostly Vikings and humans—clogged the trail. Off to the side, at least one of the trees had been felled. It sprawled among its brethren, twisted and grotesque. The bark flaked off in black sheets.

Jayna looked at me, still in Were form. "Thanks," she said. "You really helped me out there." Her ears folded down timidly against her great lupine head. I resisted the urge to pat her muzzle.

"It's what we're here for," I told her. "There's no way I could've gotten to you if Amber didn't cover my ass the whole time. Never forget, we work as a team when the fight's on. You'll come out fine as long as you remember that."

I waded out of the brush and beelined for the cart with my shredded jacket draped over it. A tarp had been tied down for some added protection over the contents. I peeled it back to reveal a pile of heavy-duty crates.

"Well, well," I mused. "What have we got here?" I wedged my fingers into a space in the slats and pried the top of the crate apart.

Christmas had come early. With a massive, shit-eating grin on my face, I peeked into all the other crates in the cart. Each one was full to the brim with assault rifles and the corresponding ammunition.

"Woohoo!" Amber whooped. I glanced down the line at her and saw she'd unearthed similar loot. "We hit the mother lode, you guys!"

"No kidding." Carefully, I closed my crates as best I could and retied the tarp on top. The remains of my jacket adorned my shoulders as a badge of honor after a successful supply outing. "I have a feeling this stuff will come in very handy."

CHAPTER TWENTY-NINE

We walked the convoy and its hard-won contents back to the church after hauling the bodies into the woods off the trail. Several of the carts had been damaged in the fight, so the going was slow, but the crates survived, and that was what mattered. I cringed a little as I considered how much fire had been thrown around inches away from live ammunition, but we'd all made it out in one piece. Amber practically danced the whole way home. She couldn't wait to take inventory.

"They're gonna be so pissed when they find out this cargo isn't coming through," she said gleefully.

I looked at the array of boxes. Now that they were in our hands, I could be thankful there were so many. But the sheer volume concerned me. "I'm not sure I want to know why those fuckers needed to be so well armed, though."

"Don't sweat it," Amber advised. "This stuff's ours now." She crowbarred the nearest crate open and lifted out boxes of ammo. "Oh man, this is going to help so much."

"Do you know where I can find the radio room?" I

asked. The size of our spoils meant that sorting through it would likely take hours, and I didn't want to get caught up in it. I'd left poor Luis hanging long enough.

"Huh?" She blinked at me and processed the question. "The radio? It's up in the bell tower. The door to the staircase is right behind the main altar. Go straight back through the sanctuary."

"Thanks," I said. "Catch you later. I need to contact some people."

She waved absently. "Good luck. The signal's not bad up there, but it's been a little finicky lately. I hope it doesn't give you too much trouble."

I took the hand radio out of my pocket as I cut through the bustle in the sanctuary. The indoor scene reminded me a lot of Fort Victory, although not quite as organized. The church's residents sat in groups, talking, eating, and laughing together. Children chased each other across the barren floor. Outside the few windows that hadn't been sealed to keep out the cold, I spotted Smitty's Weres on patrol. He'd really built a good thing for himself and Amber out in this creepy forest. I was glad for them.

The tower staircase, narrow and spiraling, looked like a set piece from a gothic movie. If I stood in the center of the ground floor and tilted my head all the way back, the massive maw of the bell yawned above me, its clapper the pupil in a great, dark eye.

Quite a feat of architecture, Marcus commented. *Clearly a remnant of purer times.*

"Yeah," I retorted. "Accusing random people of witchcraft and then burning them at the stake was *super* pure. I bet there's a god or two who are pretty mad about that one."

In my experience, there is little the gods are not angry about, Marcus said.

The climb up was long but not too difficult. I took the shallow steps two or three at a time. When I reached the top, the bell loomed above my head and a rope as thick as my arm dangled from the clapper. The juvenile urge to ring it as loud as possible gnawed at my insides. I actually reached for the rope, but pulled my hand back at the last minute.

"They'd probably think the world was ending," I told myself out loud. "It'd be worse than pulling a fire alarm."

To be fair, the world is ending, in a way, Marcus said. *Not that I condone this mischief.*

"If you stood here, you would've pulled the shit out of it," I said and smirked. "We both know the truth."

I reserve the right to say absolutely nothing.

I scanned the round, open chamber until I spotted the radio tucked against a low wall. It was much smaller and less elaborate than ours, but its basic interface was the same. A pair of ancient headphones, held together with tape, sat on top of the wall beside the device. I leaned beside them and raised the smaller talk-box to my face.

"Come in," I said. "Anyone out there?" The channel was already synced with Luis. I hoped he wasn't sleeping or distracted.

"Loud and clear," came his response after a brief pause. "I began to think you ended up in some bizarre fourth dimension. Fill me in, chief."

He got the lowdown on our current plan. "The long and

short of it is, I'm stuck waiting," I said. "As soon as I get word from the away team I'll let you know where we're headed." I felt bad that I forced the kid to wait, but the work couldn't be exciting all the time. "Cross your fingers that it won't be long."

"We're cool," Luis told me. "We've kept busy. I have a few new rides on standby when you need 'em."

I smiled. "Awesome. You're the best."

"I know," he said. "Keep in touch, all right?"

"Will do." I slipped the radio into my pocket and turned to the well-used headphones, put them on gingerly, and twisted the tuning dial. Twenty seconds of snow buzzed in my ears. "Come on," I muttered. "She's got to be around here somewhere."

"—and remember to report everything you see, people. Collective vigilance is what keeps us alive out here. We can't afford to let our guard down." Namiko's voice crackled over the air. Her cheerful tone was undercut by a deadly serious subtext.

I pressed the button. "Namiko? It's Vic."

"Hey! I wondered when I'd hear from you again. What's going on where you are? Nothing too awful, I hope."

"Actually, things have recently taken a turn for the better," I said. "I'm in Washington with Smitty's camp." I gave her the most efficient version of the details and ended on our supply coup. "I'm trying not to be too concerned about what that means for the scale of the operation we're fighting against, but the thought is there. You know how it goes."

"Yeah." She laughed wryly. "Yeah, I do. Anything you need from me?"

I tapped my fingers idly on the large plastic cup of the earphone. "Can you patch me through to the fort, please? I want to give the girls a status update."

"Sure thing. I can't guarantee the reception quality, but at least you'll get through."

"We'll manage," I said. A flurry of clicks and whirrs rushed into the earpiece. The channel dissolved into static and reformed. The next thing I heard was a chorus of two of my favorite voices.

"Hello? Vic?" I could picture Maya and Jules huddled in chairs around the clunky fort radio, their heads leaned together over the speaker. The image made me smile wider.

"Hey, you two," I said. "I'm checking in. How are things on your end?"

"They're good!" Maya sounded as chipper as ever, which I was happy for. I needed her spirits to be high. "We heard from Frank and Steph earlier today too if you can believe that. They said they're on their way back."

I arched my eyebrows. "Really? I wonder what they found."

"Beats me," Maya said. "You know Steph. She's not much of a talker."

"Even to you?" I asked.

"What?" Maya frowned. "I think we exchanged a total of three sentences."

I shook my head. "Never mind."

"I don't get it," Maya said. "Anyway, supplies are stable. We're eating well. It's as cold as hell every night now, so preserving food is way less of a problem for the moment."

"Everyone's still happy for the most part," Jules added.

"They've asked about you a couple times. I think the general consensus is that the fort is safest when you're here. But Veronica hasn't mentioned major unrest, and so far, there haven't been any riots. We're locked into the idea of wintering here."

I nodded. "There's bound to be some cabin fever, especially as the weather freezes over. I had some itchy feet myself before I left. But as long as they're all committed to ensuring the safety of the group, I think we'll come out the other side fine."

"If no one gets sick," Maya pointed out. "V and I are in the process of arranging another pharmacy run. I'd like to stock up on everything we can before cold and flu season hits. Germs will spread like the damn devil in here."

"Good idea." I sat down on the wall. "It sounds like you guys are all kicking serious butt back there. I'm proud of you."

"What about in Washington?" Jules asked. "Is everyone okay?" A subtle note of urgency rang in the question. I had a sneaking suspicion that I knew whom she was most curious about.

"Yeah," I replied, a little teasingly. "Smitty and Amber are amazing. You should see the outfit they're running here. It's in a church."

"Oh. Oh, that's great!" Jules tried hard to disguise the disappointment in her words. I felt a pang of guilt. "A church might creep me out at night, though. It sounds spooky."

"Brax is okay too," I told her. "He even smiled a few times yesterday." I conveniently left out the violent reason why.

"Wow," said Jules. "That's unusual." Even over the distance and the shoddy signal, which grew worse by the second, I knew she was flustered. The blush almost registered on the radio readout. She said something else after that, but it cut out after the first syllable.

Namiko replaced her in the headphones. "Things are starting to break up," she said. The sentence crackled. "We've got to go."

"Hey." Jules came in one more time. "Can you tell—" The static overtook the last part of her sentence. She paused and tried again. "Tell—" Again, nothing but snow followed.

I smiled slightly, and on the off chance that she could still hear me, I said, "Okay, I'll tell Brax you want to go to prom with him." An incoherent snippet of her voice popped through the noise. It sounded like she might be yelling. Then the channel cut out completely. I chuckled, removed the headset carefully, and stepped away from it to walk to the other side of the chamber and enjoy the view. A thin, cold mist blanketed the trees in soft gray. This high up, my eyes traced the scars left in the land by Oxylem and the Vikings. Evidence of the fires stood out despite the fog.

Oxylem has committed grave atrocities out of fear, Marcus mused. *But I still feel sadness for the way he must have suffered at his own hand. I have no doubt the remorse described by Jerry was genuine.*

It was hard to wrap my brain around the idea of a god shedding tears as he worked to destroy the land he loved. The more it stuck in my head, the less I wanted to think about it. I took a deep breath of the crisp, wild air and focused my eyes far out on the murky horizon. Tiny droplets of condensed water clung to my skin and clothes. "What a gorgeous place," I said. "But kind of damp, though."

"I hate it," someone grunted at my back. "Give me dry heat any day. I don't care if it's a hundred and twenty degrees in the shade." Brax propped himself up in the corner to my left.

"I figured you'd hate that kind of weather more than this," I said. "Because of Asphodel."

"I'm not saying I love it," he answered. "But it's easier to tolerate than this. It feels like I'm soaked all the time." He stared out at the view. "Nice country, I guess. I mean the part that doesn't have all the fucked-up trees."

I swallowed my smile. "Right." He fell silent and held his trademark tough-guy pose. Droplets beaded on his glasses and he eventually took them off and scowled as he stuck them into a pocket. I made sure not to stare at his naked face. "Hey, Brax, can I ask you a question? You don't have to answer, but I've wondered about it."

"What?" he asked flatly. He was obviously not thrilled, but he didn't say no.

"Laurel's baby," I began, somewhat hesitantly. "Why'd you save her?"

"We already talked about this," he answered gruffly but didn't look at me.

"Not really," I said. "You told me you were reminded of something, and that was it. I know there must be a story there."

"And let me guess, you want to hear it?" He glanced my way expectantly.

"Only if you want to tell it," I said as gently as I thought he'd allow.

For a few moments, the demon said nothing. Then he shuffled his way over to a place where he could sit and heaved a sigh. "You humans get fixated on the weirdest shit," he told me. "All right. Whatever. Here you go."

CHAPTER THIRTY

I didn't join Brax right away. He was clearly out of his comfort zone, and I wanted to give him his space. He leaned forward with his elbows on his knees and studied his clasped hands. Whenever his black eyes caught the light, they sparkled slightly, like multifaceted jewels.

"I don't know how long ago it was." He spoke after a long period of solemn contemplation. "Phoenician empire, maybe. It would've been ancient times for your kind. You were only learning how to write and all that shit." He chuckled to himself. "Anyway, it barely matters. Once upon a time, let's say, I got out of Asphodel and they couldn't catch me. Whether they forgot, or they decided to not give a shit, or they were so mad their damn heads exploded, I don't care. All I know is, I was out for a long time."

"Got it," I said.

He nodded. "In the beginning, it was impossible to enjoy freedom, even though I loved it. The feeling of going anywhere I wanted, whenever I wanted, with no one looking over my shoulder? There's nothing like it in this world or the next. But I was a fugitive, and I was never sure who lurked around the next corner. I was paranoid." His dark gaze flicked to me. "I had to be. If Kronin had sent anyone to chase my sorry ass down, I knew exactly who he would have chosen." He paused to give me a sharp look. "Would you sit down? You're making me fucking nervous standing there."

"Sorry," I said. He shifted to make a space for me, and I took it.

Brax resumed his story. "The guy's name was Belen. I called him Bell End later, which he did *not* appreciate."

That is extremely disrespectful, Marcus cut in. *Belen was not the head of a phallus.*

"If you haven't guessed, he filled the same spot as your invisible buddy, only years before. I wish I could say he loved Kronin less, but I think he might've loved him more. He was a real zealot. And a real asshole." Brax rubbed his jaw and his brow furrowed at the memory.

This slander is heinous, but I shall bear it to hear the demon's tale.

"Don't get me wrong," he clarified. "Belen was good at the things that made him valuable to Kronin. He was supremely confident, shrewd, and strong in battle and in mind. What he lacked was integrity. He'd skin me alive as soon as he'd throw me back into Asphodel if he was given the opportunity to choose. Hell, I'm sure he wanted to. Kronin had to keep him on a tight leash, or else he'd be ruthless."

I listened for Marcus's commentary. This time, the centurion stayed quiet. "You stayed away from him," I said.

Brax shrugged. "He never showed up. I spent years

constantly on the lookout and expected to see his smug, sneering face bear down on me at any second. It never happened, and the longer time went on, the more I relaxed. I let myself think I'd finally done it, and I gave myself permission to roam freely over the world. Or as freely as possible, anyway. I still wasn't able to interact with humans, on account of all this." He made a vague motion that encompassed his blatantly demonic features. "And I couldn't risk stirring up trouble, so I drifted along in the margins of society and tried to ignore the void I felt. I was weak."

"You were lonely," I suggested

He knit his brows. "Same thing. I didn't think I'd want any sort of companionship after the way I was treated in Asphodel. It hit me hard." He hesitated. "And then one day, I was hiking through the mountains on another one of my long walks to nowhere, and I heard this terrible scream straight out of hell. To this day, I can't say why, but I went to investigate. I found this woman cornered by a mountain lion. This was back when they were huge, and they had giant fangs."

"Saber teeth," I said.

"Yeah, close enough to it anyway. She was about three seconds from getting ripped apart. I jumped in and got torn up instead." He grimaced. "It was a stupid thing to do. She didn't have a scratch on her, but I was hurt. She said she couldn't leave me like that. And she took me in."

"What was her name?" Of all the things Brax might have told me, a love story was the thing I least expected. He looked ready to staunchly deny any hint of romance or soft feelings, but I could not be fooled.

"Elissa," he said. "A widow with children to care for alone. As repayment for her kindness, I took up residence on her small farm and tended to her flocks and raised her children in her late husband's stead. I'd be lying if I said I didn't grow to enjoy it. She was a warm, compassionate soul. All her little ones were bright and curious. Gentle things, those kids. We might have remained that way for a long time—the rest of their lives. It's impossible to know.

"Belen didn't stay away forever. When he finally showed himself on Elissa's land, it was to say that he had observed me, watched, and waited for a weakness to reveal itself. He patiently allowed me to form bonds with the fragile humans I came to know, and then he struck. I was ordered to comply with his every demand or see the whole region burned to the ground." Brax's face was a stone mask. "All he asked was that I give myself up and return to Asphodel. That was all he had permission to ask. If Kronin's authority hadn't tied his hands, he might have killed them regardless, simply to punish me. That's the kind of man he was, deep down.

"I've never hated anything more than I hated Belen at that moment. But I did what he said because I wanted Elissa and her children to be safe. As far as I know, he honored his end of the bargain, but that's another thing lost. My next escape was far too late. She was gone from this world, as were all traces of her family line. Belen remained. And so did I."

"Fuck," I muttered under my breath. "I'm sorry, Brax."

I, too, must offer as sincere an apology as I am able. I had no knowledge of the details of these events. Had I truly understood their gravity, perhaps I would have acted with more sensitivity. I am sorry, Abraxzael, for the cruelty of my predecessor. Belen was not a perfect man.

"It hardly seems worth fretting over now," said Brax in response to my empathy, "but I appreciate the sentiment." He moved his hand to his coat pocket, and I figured he would put his glasses back on. Instead, he withdrew a slip of paper, which he handed to me. "You wanted to know what your friend gave me. Take a look."

I unfurled the sheet. It was a poem written in Jules's precise handwriting, about a beautiful girl and the "rough" man who saved her. It was sweet. Underneath the verses, Jules had noted, *Mediterranean region, twelfth century BC?*

"Where does she find this stuff?" I folded the paper and returned it to him.

He shrugged. "It is a kinder gift than any I've received in thousands of years. Maybe the kindest gift of my lifetime." He gazed thoughtfully at the trees. "I believed what Belen said that day for all the years to follow, that caring for others is a weakness. I still want to believe it today. Things are easier with an unmoored heart."

"I used to think so, too," I told him. "Then I got thrown into this batshit crazy mess, and I learned it's exactly the opposite. Think about how fucking badass you looked, saving that family. Think about how they'll always remember what you did for them. You're building a legacy, Brax, with every incredible, selfless thing you do."

He mulled that over quietly.

"It's not a weakness," I emphasized. "We both know you're the furthest thing from weak. If I had to guess, I'd say that's why you keep jailbreaking Asphodel like it's nothing. You care, and it makes you stronger."

He remained silent, lost in thought.

"She asked about you over the radio," I said.

Brax grunted. "Good for her."

I smirked. "Okay. I wanted to let you know."

A beat passed. Then he asked, "She's doing well?"

"Yeah." I patted him on the shoulder. "She's doing really well."

CHAPTER THIRTY-ONE

We didn't come down from the bell tower wreathed in the sunshine and rainbows of best friendship, but Brax and I rejoined our team with a new, deeper understanding of each other. I was grateful that he'd displayed enough trust in me to open up and be vulnerable for the first time in countless ages. For his part, he had lost some of his permanently sullen aura. Although he didn't say so, I was sure he liked to know that Jules was thinking about him.

And the small blessings continued to pile up. Given our track record for such things, I half-expected to descend to some type of chaos in the church. Another fire or the roof caving in. What we found was a slew of soldiers doing a painstaking inspection of the equipment from the caravan. The one in charge had a clipboard in her hand on which she recorded notes about every individual weapon.

"You look busy," I said to her. "I told Amber she could call me if she needed help."

The soldier laughed. "Oh, she ran off to do some more

espionage a while ago. Besides, this isn't hard work, merely tedious. We're used to this kind of thing."

I glanced around for Smitty and didn't see him either. "Well, we might as well make ourselves useful." Brax and I stationed ourselves at an available crate and sifted through boxes of bullets. My mind still reeled a little from the demon's tale but gradually settled into the comfortable humdrum of menial tasks. I got into a rhythm—pick up a box, note the brand, number, and type of bullets, repeat. If there wasn't anything on the packaging, I made my best guess. Neither one of us talked, but we didn't feel the need to. Brax had already said more words than I'd ever heard out of his mouth.

The dull tranquility of the afternoon shattered as the doors to the church flew open and banged against the stone walls. Smitty's white Were form hurtled across the threshold toward me. The ridge between his shoulders was raised, every hair on end. Dark streaks of blood matted his fur.

"Come quickly!" he roared, and his voice echoed through the sanctuary. "Amber's in danger. She's been taken."

Brax and I both leapt to our feet. "What the fuck?" I spouted incredulously.

Smitty was fairly frothing at the mouth. "She was far behind enemy lines, deeper than she's been before. Lord knows what the girl heard to make her go that way, but she was ambushed in the trees. That fool Oxylem has her strung up somewhere."

"He's soft-hearted, but he's not stupid," Brax said.

"Oxylem has eyes everywhere. It'd be more surprising if he didn't know about her by now."

"My granddaughter is in mortal danger," Smitty bellowed. "Her radio broadcasted for a while after the attack. I heard the son of a bitch castigating her for using wolves against him and turning 'nature against nature' or some cockamamie shit. He sentenced her to a public execution." The blacksmith's wild gaze rolled from face to face. "Please. We can't leave her to die. She's all the family I have left."

"Okay." I grabbed one of his massive paws in both my hands. "Just breathe for a minute. Clear your head so you can think rationally. Amber needs that from you. We'll figure this out."

Smitty huffed and shook himself vigorously. "If they kill her…" he growled.

"They won't," I said. "I refuse to let that happen."

Victoria, wait a moment. If we abandon our current plan to attack Delano's forces in search of Amber, we run a great risk of alerting him to our presence, thus destroying our entire objective. I need not remind you what is at stake here. Delano's machinations have spread across the world.

"We need to do something, Vic," Smitty urged. "Now! I won't gamble with Amber's life."

I looked at Brax. His glasses were firmly in place and his face had become the blank canvas I was used to—except that his fists were clenched and his jaw was set. He knew the stakes as well as I did. Our goals, I was sure, were essentially the same. And yet, it was painfully obvious what he wanted to do.

He had sacrificed himself for a woman he cared about

once. Now, he was willing to do it again. Maybe not so much for his own sake as for Smitty's, but still. The guy deserved credit.

"It's a trap," he said and made eye contact with me. "She walked into it. He's using her as bait to goad us into attacking."

"Delano might be there already," I said. "He might've been there all along and simply bided his time until we made a mistake."

"This is not Amber's fault," Smitty snapped. "She did nothing she hasn't done a hundred times before." His harsh, beast voice had cracks in it. Tears glistened in his fierce eyes. "They got lucky this once, and I'll make them pay."

"We might be walking to the slaughter," Brax told him. "There's no telling what's waiting for us when we get to wherever Oxylem wants us to go. We can't act like this is a predictable situation. He's not in his right mind."

Smitty blew up. "None of that matters to me, boy! Don't you understand? Those monsters have my little girl in their filthy clutches, and—" He swallowed hard. "And—"

"No, I understand," the demon said quietly. "We will bring her back safe and sound. I promise you. That said, I feel it would be irresponsible to rush in without acknowledging that the whole situation is designed to ensnare us. We have to be ready for anything."

One by one, they all turned to me. A soldier came up and tapped me on the shoulder. "You'll need this," she said and handed me the *Gladius Solis* in its sheath. I placed it back on my belt. The comfort of its solid weight made me feel more powerful already.

"He wants us to come after him?" I asked Brax. "Do you feel strongly about this?"

"Absolutely," he answered. "He could have caught her innumerable times before this moment. As clever and quick as she is, she's no match for a god. This was orchestrated, either by Oxylem himself or by someone pulling the strings."

Smitty turned to me and bowed his grizzled head. "Please, Vic," he pleaded. "I trust you to make the decision, but it has to be made now. Amber adores you. I know she believes you're gonna come get her. Please don't let her down."

I looked into his eyes and around at the huddle that had formed while we debated. "You heard these guys," I said and lifted my sword. "Let's give Oxylem what he fucking wants. For Amber!"

"For Amber!" they echoed. The sanctuary drowned in warlike howls as the Weres transformed for battle and swarmed toward the exit after their white-furred leader. They poured down the staircase and loped in the direction of the black, thorny trees. Right at their furry heels, Brax and I kept pace and brought up the rear with flaming hammer and burning sword. Once again, the ashes of our plans lay trampled beneath our feet.

This time, I wasn't that upset about it.

"You want some, Delano?" I muttered. "Then how about you come and fucking get it?"

CHAPTER THIRTY-TWO

We determined quickly that it would be best for me to go in alone at first. Other than a general idea of where we'd find it, no one had any real details about the gods' base of operations. I was the one with the god-killing sword, so I took point. Only Marcus was with me as I headed down the uneven track toward the heart of the forest.

"I will be pissed if we find out they set up another slaughterhouse-type deal," I said. "That place still haunts my dreams."

It should hold a special place in your heart, Marcus said, with the same inflection as a proud parent. *That was your first major proving ground.*

"You always put the weirdest spin on things," I told him as I shook my head. The trees closed in tighter with every step until I felt like I pushed my way through a loosely knit blanket of dead sticks and leaves. I hacked through it with a regular machete from the church. Yeah, I was on my way to use the hell out of my huge, glowing sword, but there was no point in blowing it early. If I had a chance at the element of surprise, I wanted to seize it.

Inspiration is an art, Marcus declared. *And I am a master.*

A wooden barrier snapped and crunched in front of me as I struck it. A hole opened, and I was blasted with a current of cold, wet air. I lined my fist up with the opening and punched outward with all my might. The dense wall caved in, and I stepped through into a new path, much wider and cleaner. The walls on either side of this passage were crude but deliberate in design, made of what looked to be the same dark, corrupted wood that filled the woods around me.

I whistled softly. "They were harvesting trees for material? Damn. Smitty said these used to be humans."

Not always humans, but living creatures of flesh and bone, yes. Now they are... He trailed off, unwilling or unable to voice the thought.

"Yeah," I said. "This shit's fucked."

At the end of the long, dark passage, a massive wall jutted up into the darkness. Some of the boards on the outside were so fresh, I could smell the cut wood as I approached. Rudimentary parapets lined the top. Through the gaps, I discerned the shapes of waiting soldiers. Others ran back and forth along the elevated footpath, apparently still slapping the fortification together. Wooden planks clattered into place, followed by the bang of hammers.

"I guess we're a little early," I said. "Let's see if they could use a hand in there."

They appear to be reinforcing the outer wall, Marcus

observed. *It would seem they consider an invasion to be imminent.*

I chuckled. "They're not wrong. I'm basically a one-woman invasion, wouldn't you say? And there will be hell to pay once Smitty gets through."

When I reached the end of the path, I slowed my pace. The wall's construction had obviously been hurried. The boards and planks were often rough and unaligned. I spotted a plethora of potential handholds dotting the wooden surface. They were full of potential splinters and bristled with nails, but they'd do.

"That's it," I announced. "We're going over. On my mark." I dropped into a sprinter's starting stance. "Three... two... one!" My whole body shot forward, powered by nectar, adrenaline, and grit. I was on the wall and scaled that thing like an angry lizard before the guards up top began to shout about an intruder.

"Too late, assholes," I muttered and pushed myself to climb faster. Gunshots peppered the air over my head. A bullet slammed into the wood two inches from my right hand, gouged a trough down the wall, and spattered sawdust into my eyes. I squinted and pressed on.

The muzzle flashes, which started as pinpricks in the vertical distance, rapidly grew larger. I clawed from perch to perch and dodged hails of bullets. The gunmen never missed by very much. One or two shots grazed me to leave thin trickles of blood. The skin of my palms had split from hastily grabbing un-sanded ledges. I paid no attention to any of that.

I was too focused on the serious ass I intended to kick once I reached the top. I'd never been more pumped for a fight than I was at that moment. Maybe it was the exhilaration of throwing our plans to the wind. Maybe it was because I knew Amber was there somewhere and waited for us to find her.

Or maybe I was merely sick of this shit.

Whatever the reason for the extra energy that coursed through my veins, I vaulted up onto the top of the wall like a human hurricane and sliced burning arcs through the air with my sword. The men directly in front didn't stand a snowball's chance in Hell. Their bodies tumbled toward the ground in pieces before they could even yell for backup.

The others lunged to knock me down, but months of Marcus's meticulous training had given me incredible balance. I nimbly sidestepped the chaotic assault, cut through one, and sent the other after his doomed companion with a well-placed boot to the back. Then, I bolted along the wall in search of a way in.

At first glance, there wasn't much to help me. The base itself stood way back against a legion of yet more trees, but I was separated from it by a barren, burned-out expanse. Stumps and tree husks littered the ground. In some places, the gray ash looked deep and pooled in impressions left by countless feet. More workers hunched on the inside of the wall, building up its strength. They were men like the tree gangs, and like the gangs, most were desperately thin. It was no surprise that Delano and his cronies were big on slave labor.

Another bullet whizzed past my ear. I glanced over my shoulder long enough to glimpse more guards rushing toward my position. They seemed unsettled as if they didn't want to fight so far off the ground and were afraid of falling. But their faces also showed the same determination I had, the same fierce loyalty. Too bad they'd chosen the wrong side.

Watch out, Victoria!

Marcus's warning refocused my attention ahead, and I saw that the surface I ran on dipped down into the well of a parapet in fifteen feet. I stopped abruptly and spun to face my pursuers. Behind them, the whole nearest section of the wall now stood empty. They'd consolidated a whole section of their force to confront me.

I grinned. Big mistake.

The leader of the pack had changed from a frightened young soldier to a tall, slender man whose eyes burned with an eerily recognizable unearthly light. He was the first vamp I'd seen in quite a while with that kind of strength, and he was hungry.

His lips peeled back to reveal the vicious points of his fangs, and he launched into a blur. I stood firm, my blade out. Seconds later, the vamp was on me. He was stronger than any of the stragglers I had battled since leaving New York, and we grappled back and forth. No words were exchanged, only a few choice snarls. The skin on his gaunt face was so pale I could see a map of veins and arteries on his cheeks. He gripped my arms like a vise and tried to toss me off the side. The *Gladius Solis* wavered between us.

His movements were rigid and almost clumsy as he tried to avoid the sword so close to his flesh. I waited for his balance to shift and jerked my knee into his stomach. He buckled with a cry of pain, and I threw all my weight to the right. When the vamp scrabbled to keep his hold on my forearm, I simply cut his hand off. I pried the clutching, disembodied fingers from my sleeve and flung it to the rest of the soldiers who had formed a line to block the way forward.

"Who's next?" I asked.

CHAPTER THIRTY-THREE

The vamp guard's men were brave enough to step forward even after they'd seen the first of their squad plunge to his death, but they weren't good enough to survive. I dispatched every one of them as neatly as possible, sheathed my sword, and stepped into the parapet among scattered bloodstains and dispersing ash.

The vamp presence there became more and more apparent. A sure sign, I thought, that Delano must be somewhere around. The vamps, after all, had been his first inheritance from Lorcan.

I crouched in the shadow of the wall and studied the burned field keenly. The bulk of the distant forest was obscured by a horribly ugly building, a brutal, mashed-together conglomerate made almost entirely of massive hunks of wood. Jagged angles jutted out all over and gave the place a cruel, primitive air. Hospitality had not been a concern during its construction, that much was certain.

The other thing that caught my attention was the sheer number of enemies who rambled around down there. They were doing something and rushed around like evil little ants. Most looked like humans or fire Vikings, but some towered over the rest and moved with lanky, long-limbed grace. These tall ones had thick, dark skin that covered most of their bodies, and the greater their height, the slower they moved.

"What the hell am I looking at?" I asked aloud.

Giants, Marcus said. *The oldest of Oxylem's followers. Perhaps the last remnants of his former glory. They, too, have fallen to dark influence, it seems.*

A commotion had broken out far back at the edge of the woods, where ranks of marching people now emerged. In the very front, a fire soldier walked stiffly with hundreds of lumber slaves at his back. A cacophony of jeers enveloped me on every side and erased all other sounds. The effect was suffocating as if I'd shut myself into a slowly shrinking box. Harsh laughter scraped at my ears. Weapons were lifted and shaken, as well as fists.

But the pandemonium stopped as abruptly as it had started. There was something wrong with the scene that unfolded. The fire Viking had moved close enough for spectators to realize that his hands were bound tightly behind his back and manacles were clamped around his ankles. Some of the woodsmen had chains too, but theirs were broken.

A rift appeared near the middle of the crowd and advanced rapidly toward the front line. I identified Brax's sturdy, unflinching stride before he reached the trapped soldier and pushed him squarely between the shoulder blades. The man stumbled. The demon gripped his upper arm, and I watched him drag his quarry toward the middle of the cleared plain.

Nobody jeered now. All the personnel in or near the wall, even the ones who could get to Brax, stood frozen and simply stared. I wondered why they didn't attack.

A voice rang out from the foot of the wall. "This is madness!" It was the voice of an elderly man, the kind that creaks and groans with every syllable. A lone figure broke away from the wall with a small crew at his heels. He stopped halfway to Brax and turned back toward me for a moment.

Marcus drew in a breath. *Oxylem?*

I frowned. "I thought someone said he was young." The god in front of me was ancient, shriveled, and drooped visibly. Hair that might once have been a brilliant shade of gold hung limply around his drawn, ashen face with the quality of tarnished brass. Dark circles and lines marred his crumpled skin. A strong wind might have blown him over.

He was young, Marcus said quietly. *He has always been the epitome of beauty and youth. This? I do not know what to say.*

"It looks like the price of evil is pretty damn steep," I remarked. "I'm surprised he's still hanging in there."

It is a tragic situation, said Marcus. *But it is also clear to me that nothing more can be done, regardless of who he used to be. His path has been chosen, along with his fate.*

I adjusted my grip on the *Gladius Solis*. "That sounds like you've given me the go-ahead to kill him. And I'm merely letting you know that I won't argue if that's the case."

Wait. Let us allow this scenario to play out first. I am sure Abraxzael has engineered things this way for a reason.

I smirked. "Look at you, suddenly keeping the demon faith. I'm proud of you." But I left my sword bladeless and kept my eyes on Brax. He showed no indication of being affected in any way by Oxylem's words. He hadn't even removed his glasses. "How the fuck does he still have those?" At the very least, I would've assumed they'd get knocked off his face by now.

The Marked work in mysterious ways.

Oxylem's voice raised again and carried over the battered field. "Madness!" he repeated. "Do you not remember what happened the last time you tried to resist? Your accursed people died by the thousands. What makes you think they will not do so again?" The god looked at everyone assembled, his withered features fixed in a mask of stony resignation. "There is no light. There is no hope. It was the werewolves who began this futile struggle, then abandoned it in the throes of cowardice. Let them be the ones to end it, not you."

Brax didn't move a muscle except to open his mouth. "If you insist," was all he said.

At that precise moment, the trees behind Oxylem's brutish fort sent up their distinctive, chilling howl. The god fidgeted where he stood, apparently startled. I couldn't keep the grin off my face as Smitty and his forces barreled out of the woods, more of them than I'd ever seen in one place. The Weres were monstrous tanks of muscle and claw and tooth. Their raw, wild energy colored the atmosphere and churned the air. Most of the guards and soldiers drew away from them instinctually. They rose in silence behind Smitty, angry and not to be fucked with.

I loved them so much.

For the third time, Oxylem turned toward me and directed his eyes at what I assumed was a gate in the wall. He motioned with his hand, and two more guards marched out with a human strung between them. She writhed and kicked, and her hair flashed with every movement.

"That has to be Amber," I muttered.

Yes, Marcus affirmed. *And make no mistake, Oxylem is no longer the soft soul he once was. She is far from safe.*

She was dropped at the god's feet where she lay on her side, her arms and legs bound. He didn't touch her, but he did raise a wooden spear and pointed the tip directly at her heart. "I will only say this once," he proclaimed. His voice was heavy but firm. "Stand down immediately, or this young creature will die before your eyes." His tone softened slightly. "Take solace in the fact that she will make a beautiful tree, a thousand-year monument to the chaos you have wrought."

He lifted his narrow chin as his fingers tightened on the haft of the spear. Amber squirmed. The spear inched closer to her.

"Well, beasts?" Oxylem prompted. "Time runs short."

Brax and Smitty were statues in front of the slaves they had freed. As frantic as he had been earlier, the old blacksmith's composure remained hard as a rock. They looked at each other, and Smitty nodded. I held my breath.

The demon forced the Viking soldier to his knees and crushed his skull with one decisive blow. In response,

Oxylem jerked his spear back and prepared to plunge it into Amber's heart.

Strike now! Marcus commanded.

In a fraction of a second, I lit my blade and thrust it from me. The sword swept downward and blazed toward the back of Oxylem's shoulder. It struck beneath the joint. His arm, relieved of its attachment to the rest of his body, spun off at an angle. The god collapsed into the anxious arms of his men, and the sword arced to return to me and severed her bonds in the process. As the ropes fell onto the charred ground, the feisty Amber clambered to her feet and dashed toward her grandfather's fearsome ranks. The werewolves surged forward to meet her.

The *Gladius Solis* returned to my hand in time to be brandished at the swarms of guards that angled directly toward me.

I smiled. The battle was officially on.

CHAPTER THIRTY-FOUR

They hit me like a tidal wave as their hands grabbed and feet kicked. I planted my feet down hard and lashed out with the sword again and again. The ambient light of the blade lit their faces, and I saw more vamps among them. Fighting those guys gave me a weird sense of nostalgia for the early New York days and all the trouble I got into following Rocco Durant around the seediest parts of town. These slimeballs probably had no idea who he was.

The guards on the wall were fast and strong, but they weren't particularly suited for hand-to-hand combat in such close quarters. I had innumerable opportunities to shove them off the edge, and I used every chance I got. The swinging arcs of my blade made short work of their fleshy bodies. One idiot actually attempted to grab its cutting edge with his gloved hand, as if the thin material would be enough to save him. He screamed when his hand was instantly vaporized by the heat.

"Really, dude?" I asked prior to running him through

the gut. He died with an expression of pained confusion frozen onto his face.

As my opponents fell, I looked to the left and right and gauged the number of new challengers. The wall, which had been sparsely populated a second ago, now crawled with a zillion soldiers all after my blood. Gunfire picked up again in earnest, and I took that as my cue to reach lower ground. I dropped from the floor of the parapet, swung across the face of the wall, and landed on my feet inside, thirty yards from the gate through which Oxylem had been dragged.

"Shit," I said. "This might not have been the best idea."

An even greater number of enemies clogged the field and formed a seething, impenetrable barrier. The wall rattled from a hundred impacts as Smitty's Weres leapt over the top in pursuit of screeching guards. Viking weapons battered at me from all angles except the very back, and flames seared my face.

"Yep. Bad idea," I said. The sword parried a volley of strikes and sliced through hammers, axes, and burly Viking arms. Drops of their vital fire splashed across the ground, but it was so dead already that the flames didn't catch.

Go toward the gate, Marcus urged. *It may provide you with the most reliable means of escape.*

"That's the plan," I said. No way could I ever fight my way out of a mess this big. With every step, more bodies crushed around me like a living tomb. When they tried to circle to my back, I thrust the sword out and spun, which spattered me with blood, Viking embers, and vamp ash. I kept my lips tightly closed lest any of that gross shit get in my mouth. The thought alone made me want to puke.

"Get her," someone roared and injected new vigor into the bloodthirsty mob. Suddenly, it seemed like the hands that grasped for purchase on my clothes and body had doubled in number. Luckily, I had become very good at cutting them off.

For every soldier who fell away, five more appeared and charged at me in a frenzy. This army was like a thousand hydras. I could feel the nectar working overtime to push me through. "Man, this will hurt in the morning," I said. "Is there a massage therapist on call at the church?"

My back hit something that rattled and gave and a latticework of wooden stakes pressed against my spine. Finally, the gate. I stared into the murderous faces of a dozen beasts who thought they were inches from killing me, smiled, and aimed the sword in a new direction.

The lock shattered on contact and allowed the gate panel to swing open. I stood motionless in the flood of furious Weres and freed slaves that poured through. My attackers were swept away in a stampede of rifle fire and ferocious mauling.

Brax brought up the rear and caught me by the shoulder. "It looked a little hairy for a minute there," he remarked with a grin. "Good thing I came to save you."

I rolled my eyes, even though he was more right than usual. "I still can't believe you managed to hide all those guns on your person." I glanced at the woodsmen shooting with wild abandon into the teeming mass of soldiers. "I think they're enjoying them."

"Who wouldn't?" Brax asked. He was as close to outright cheerful as I'd ever seen him. "I'm like that Christmas demon who eats all the shitty kids." Mid-sentence, he brought the head of his hammer down on the head of an incredibly unfortunate vamp who approached from the side. He swung the weapon under and launched the fresh corpse into the brawl forcibly enough to send more sprawling. "I don't even have to try." He had a satisfied smile on his face before he loped away again to prove the point by beating a path through the violence.

I dove in headfirst, eager for a bigger slice of the action. The Viking weapons had torn the field up, and freezing muck coated everything from the shins down. I drew the warmth and energy of the *Gladius Solis* into my body and whirled through the battle. The vamps and woodsmen were cut down in droves. They mingled with the ashes already strewn across the mud.

Vikings were a slightly bigger problem, both in stature and strategy. For once, the general wetness of the day helped as it prohibited torrents of fire-blood from spreading. The brutes could pack one hell of a wallop, but it was hard for their slow asses to catch me as I literally ran circles around them. The sword's unbreakable rope trick came in handy. I left them bundled into bales in my wake. They were easy prey for kill-hungry Weres after that.

Still, the numbers remained damn high on both sides. I'd caught my second wind, but I began to wonder how long the onslaught would continue and if it was really endless. The confusion only increased as everyone was covered in more dirt and mud. A few isolated blazes sprang up and caused a haze of smoke to descend upon us. Despite these difficult conditions, the fight continued to rage.

I worked my way back toward the outskirts and

remained vigilant for any familiar faces. I'd long since lost sight of both Smitty and Brax, and there was one face I had yet to see at all. The concern pushed at me, so I climbed the wall once more. Up top, I hacked through challenger after challenger and almost didn't notice a hand that fell on my arm. When I did, I nearly cut it off. Then I looked up and saw the man it was attached to.

"There you are," Deacon said, slightly out of breath. "Please don't chop off my body parts. I need them more than ever right now." He wielded a gigantic ax lifted off one of the Vikings. It wasn't on fire, but it made him look hot as all hell.

"Sorry," I said sheepishly. "On the plus side, 'sexy lumberjack' is a great look for you. All you're missing is the hipster beard. And the flannel."

"Yeah?" He stroked his chin. "I think I might have missed my calling on the west coast. Maybe I should stay. Drink a lot of artisanal coffee and get some glasses with no lenses in 'em."

I laughed and reveled in the feeling of having him back at my side. But the joy of our reunion was interrupted by a shrill cry of an alarm. We shared a glance and broke into a dead run toward the top of the wall. What we saw caused a stone to grow in the pit of my stomach. Hundreds more soldiers, on foot and armed, rushed into the clash from the woods outside the gate.

"That son of a bitch," I griped. "How many troops does he have?"

"Don't worry about it," Deacon said calmly. "Look close. They're all from the lumber gangs. The enemy will get stomped."

That was the instant I noticed something else that rolled in from the trees on the heels of Oxylem's surprise contingent. "They're not the only ones," I said.

Luis drove at the helm of a platoon of vehicles, each carrying a squadron of mobile gunners. The trucks split into two wings at the gate and flanked the sides of the fortification.

"Check that kid out," I told Deacon proudly. "All those lessons have paid off."

He pretended to wipe a tear from his eye. "They grow up so fast." He turned as the first of the trucks opened fire. "I think we've got things covered here. I hate to see you go, but someone has to take care of Oxylem, and we all know who that will be."

"It's okay." I squeezed his shoulder. "At least you'll have the pleasure of watching me leave."

Deacon winked. "I *do* love that."

CHAPTER THIRTY-FIVE

I climbed down the wall and dropped the last few feet. The moment I touched down, I searched for anything that might clue me into Oxylem's whereabouts. He had been pulled this way by his lackeys, I knew that for sure, but it was hard to pick up their trail with the dirt all chewed up from fighting. Simple shit like footprints was out of the question. I dropped low to the ground and scanned the detritus for anything I could link to the god.

At face value, it seemed like a hopeless task. The whole area surrounding Oxylem's base had transformed into a war zone. In his current debilitated condition, how could I know which blood was his or which sticks were broken by his escape? No doubt, his crew would be gone by now—something told me he wouldn't run for his life with an entourage.

Refusing to be defeated in my search for the tree god, I headed in the same direction in which Luis had sent a faction of his vehicles—around the side. I had a hunch that a wall this rushed couldn't possibly enclose the entire area, and about fifty yards into the thick woods off to the right, I found what I was looking for. In their mad rush to fend off the army they knew was coming, Oxylem's men hadn't built a complete circle.

That or the trucks had busted through a weak point. I didn't know, and I didn't care. The important thing was that I could now wind back across the battlefield toward the second thatch of forest behind the building. I was willing to stake my life that he hid there among the last tragic dregs of all he hadn't been able to save.

The trees weren't as dense alongside the battlefield as they had been elsewhere. The rampant clearcutting had extended into these tracts of forest and left sizable gaps. I had a good view of the ongoing fight on my way past. The tide seemed to turn in our favor. Oxylem's men, severely weakened, were falling back.

But his men didn't matter to me as much as the god himself. I couldn't let that half-wilted bastard slip through my fingers. I did my best to keep a low profile and avoid being drawn into the battle that still raged and increased my pace. Focused now, I raced toward the back of the hideous fortress. A lapse in tree coverage forced me to dart through the open, the sword hilt tucked safely out of sight, but I was soon immersed in the trees once more. The sounds of war grew muffled behind me.

After a moment, I slowed. It was easy to be surprised while running, and it was as easy for tunnel vision to set in. The god could be anywhere, so I had to stay vigilant.

I wound around a bend and reached the edge of a small clearing in which pale, blurred figures moved about. The noises that reached my ears weren't even close to human, merely growls and screams. I drew the *Gladius Solis* and stole up to the edge of the trees for a better look. As I did, a different scream pierced the hush of the woods. This one was much, much closer to what I was used to. Someone was trapped.

I ran in, poised to strike, and stopped dead in my tracks. Oxylem cowered amid a pack of creatures I'd never seen before and attempted weakly to fend them off. His clothes were tattered, and shreds of material lay where the beasts had torn them and let them fall. Bruises bloomed on his grayish skin. His eyes locked on to mine, filled to the brim with panic. The creatures noticed his gaze and turned curiously to see what had barged in on their little party.

"What the fuck is this nonsense?" I asked.

The translucent, waxy skin, the bloodshot eyes, and the protruding fangs told me these things were vampires, but they had virtually nothing in common with the vamps back east or the ones in the rest of the compound. They were beefier, although they moved with a grace that implied speed, and the gnashing teeth in their mouths were huge and fearsome—the kind of mandibles that would rip out an entire esophagus, no problem. Their heavy lower jaws protruded, which might have been a little funny if I wasn't so sure they could kill the shit out of me.

The closest one faced me and hissed through its teeth. Flecks of foamy saliva flung from its mouth. Its shoulders raised, and a pair of disturbingly muscular, flesh-toned wings unfurled. Each of the five long fingers on its hands ended in a ragged claw.

To top it all off, they had tails. Pointy, barbed tails lashed around their feet like snakes.

"This is wrong," I said. "Everything about this is wrong. What the hell happened to them?"

Your guess is as good as mine, Marcus said. His voice carried a hint of revulsion. *For now, I suggest you save your concern for what is about to happen to you.*

The freak vamps circled like vultures closing in on a carcass. Nothing remotely resembling language passed through their throats, but they watched me with sharp, unsettling intelligence.

I did a quick headcount. "Eight," I said. "Cool. This is gonna be interesting."

The vamps I had gotten to know and love were fond of mobbing and overwhelmed through numbers. It was a technique I learned to embrace because their enthusiasm only served to make my job easier. In stark contrast, these new guys were in no hurry to attack. They remained at a distance, observing and calculating. I could sense the gears turning in their heads.

What they were thinking, I could only guess.

My knowledge of these monstrosities is nonexistent, Marcus warned. *I will do my best to be of technical assistance, but we have ventured into truly unknown territory, perhaps for the first time.*

I shrugged. "It was bound to happen sooner or later."

Whenever I spoke, the neo-vamps watched my mouth move. They had completely abandoned their original target. Oxylem shivered, reluctant to move. He said nothing.

"What?" I looked at each of the monsters. "Now that I'm here, you'll make me wait? Let's get this over with." I paused to really absorb their appearance. "Holy shit, you guys are ugly. I've seen week-old roadkill with more charm."

My brazen insults worked. The trio in the front raised their hackles and displayed even more of their impressive dentistry. I assumed a fighting stance as their grotesque bodies coiled low for a spring.

Three of them released at the same time and flew directly at me. The angle made them appear huge, and I barely spun out of the way in time. One of them caught my poor, embattled jacket on those nasty claws and left a good-sized rend in the fabric.

I danced to the left. "Good thing distress is in style."

Their next strikes glanced off the burning blade of my sword, and they hissed in pain from the blisters on their skin. That brought some satisfaction, but I noticed that the other five had gradually tightened the circumference of their circle. They hunted me the same way pack animals hunted prey. If I slipped up too badly, I was done for.

Prioritize your targets, said Marcus. *Focus on individuals instead of the group at large. It is the only way to keep from becoming overwhelmed. Take a deep breath. You can do this.*

The medallion warmed against my sternum. It made me smile.

"I learned from the best," I said. I set my sights on the central vamp and got down to business. It backed up in preparation for another attack. I didn't dare close the distance myself. That would leave me vulnerable on either side. Instead, I hung back and exercised patience in an effort to draw out the aggression. A striking enemy, I had discovered through much trial and error, was more likely to make a mistake.

But that didn't happen. The vamps peppered me with manageable but more or less constant blows designed to wear me down, make me tired, and force me to slip. They obviously wanted to rip me open right then and there, but instincts—and possibly training—told them to take the slow and steady route. It was infinitely more frustrating. I matched them to the best of my ability until I couldn't take it anymore. I was unscathed, and this was a waste of time. Oxylem now crept toward the perimeter of the clearing.

I could not afford to lose him.

"Can we maybe speed this up a little?" I asked the vamps. "I have somewhere I need to be."

They didn't care. All they wanted was to continue their obnoxious pattern until I gave them the chance to incapacitate me. I'd seen it dozens of times on nature programs in the days when I still had tv. The crucial difference was that the prey in those shows didn't have swords. I'd used mine for defense long enough.

It was time to switch to an offensive play.

The next volley proceeded as usual. I fended the vamps on the sides off with a deft hand and turned fluidly to block each of their attempts. The one in the center leapt at me, braced for the blade, and expected to be knocked back. This time, I hooked the sword under and jabbed at the vamp's unguarded abdomen. With the move, I risked a brutal eyeful of claws. Their very tips scratched along my cheekbone, but the pain was such a shock that it caused the vamp to curl up by reflex. It screeched, and I twisted the blade.

In lieu of ash, a torrent of thick, blackened blood spurted from the wound. I made a face. "What the hell kind of vamp doesn't turn to dust when it dies?" The only answer I received was in the form of a lethal tail that whipped toward my face. "Oh, shit!" The sword sliced it neatly in half. More blood fountained out. The orphaned tip twitched on the ground. "Gross."

I looked at the vamp, who had slid off the end of the blade. Its hands opened and closed, and the eyes dulled rapidly. When it finally died, the others stood motionless as if in shock for a long moment.

Then they all sought vengeance at once.

This was the fight I'd wanted all along. The *Gladius Solis* had an amazing reach when I was crowded. Some of them left the ground to hover awkwardly directly above my head as they slashed downward at my face and eyes. I ducked, aimed, and sliced a wing. That vamp crashed to the ground and knocked against another as it fell. I ran them through while they stumbled to regain their footing. As I straightened, I slashed a third out of the air. The severed wing dropped into the mud and its former owner shrieked.

The vamps became less intimidating with their foolproof strategy in shambles. But that didn't make them physically weaker. Whatever Delano had done to cook these hybrids up was way more effective than feeding them human blood alone. They couldn't be outfoxed, backed into a corner, or turned on one another. They thought fast and acted faster. They communicated and worked as a team. I had to pick each of them off, one by one, and not allow them to rally. At the end of seven out of eight, I was bloodied, tired, and madder than a fight had ever made me.

"I don't have fucking time for this!" I shouted at the last vamp. "Just die already, you sack of shit." It lifted off clumsily and hooked around to try for a divebomb. "Oh, come on!"

I tracked it through the air, and when it reared back to swoop down, I ran forward, jumped, and dragged it down by its leg. It thrashed for freedom and gashed my arm badly, but I hardly noticed. I severed its head, dropped the carcass, and looked for Oxylem. I expected him to be gone, but the weirdo lurked a few feet into the trees and simply watched me.

He fled the moment he realized the last vamp was dead.

"Damn it to hell!" I burst out. "Get back here, you shit-faced creep." He didn't stop, so I gave chase and cursed the whole way.

CHAPTER THIRTY-SIX

The woods ended without much warning on a bald, rocky shore that sloped down to the gray ocean. Oxylem was still a good way ahead and hurried to a dinghy moored on the water. He had a hell of a time untying the ropes with a single arm, but he was lucky. I was too shocked by the rest of the scene to pay attention to what he did.

The god and the dinghy were dwarfed by the massive ships that moored offshore, shrouded in the fog. They took up the entire view for as far as I could see and filled the sky with rigging, masts, and sails. Each smooth, dark-wood hull gleamed, even in the dull light. I stared, dumbstruck by the enormity of the fleet—and the realization that we'd found the reason for that massive lumberyard operation. The grain of the wood reminded me of skin in a weird way that made my stomach turn.

Victoria! Oxylem is trying to escape.

I snapped back to the moment and jogged along the shore. Choppy waves lapped restlessly at the bottom of the much smaller boat. Oxylem had the end of the hitching rope in his hand, the knot half undone. Tiny green buds sprouted from the stump under his shoulder.

"That's a neat little party trick," I called and pointed to the regrowth. "I bet it's gotten you out of a whole bunch of scrapes. It won't get you out of this one."

He whirled and promptly lost his balance and fell to his knees in the cold surf. I ambled up to him and placed the tip of the sword beneath his chin. Oxylem's lip trembled.

"Please don't," he whimpered and reached his hand toward me. He still held the boat's rope in shaking fingers. "Please let me go." His watery blue eyes swam with tears. "I have to go."

"Uh-uh." I shook my head. "I decide who goes where because I'm the one with the blade and both my arms. You'll stay put until you tell me everything that's going on here."

Oxylem blinked. A few of the tears, huge and crystalline, spilled over onto his sallow cheeks. "He forced me," he said in a hoarse whisper. "All of it. He forced me to do everything. All those—" His voice cracked, and he choked up. "All those trees. All that ugliness. I didn't want to!" The god clenched his fist. A bout of near-hysteria washed over him. "Of course I didn't want to. They were my friends!"

"But you did," I said. "Why?"

Oxylem was weeping now. "I had no choice. You don't understand. You're a human. You could never understand."

I moved the sword closer to his skin. His Adam's apple bobbed as he swallowed hard. "Try me," I told him. "I might surprise you."

"Please," he pleaded. "I have to leave. If he finds me here, he'll kill me." His eyes rolled in their sockets as he tried to look around without moving his head.

"I could kill you, too," I reminded him. "And I've already found you here. Not him."

A frigid chuckle sounded behind me. "I would think twice about that if I were you."

I whipped around and brought my sword up. It wasn't enough. One strong blow knocked me aside. It wasn't enough to send me sprawling, but the breath left my lungs.

I regained my footing on the rocks and raised my head.

"Delano?" I asked.

"Hello, darling." Lorcan's Apprenti stood before me, a far cry from the slender, pale-eyed man I remembered. He was glorious now in a terrible way, beautiful and cruel. Black wings adorned his shoulders and arched over a sharp, dark suit. The back half of his body was constantly wreathed in shifting shadows, and when he lifted his hand to brush an invisible speck of dust from his sleeve, I noticed that delicate scales now covered his skin. He examined Oxylem through cat's eyes, the pupils little more than diamond slits.

The tree god shrank down, away from Delano's reach. But the Apprenti moved with feline speed, seized him by the neck, and lifted him like a ragdoll. Delano's jaw unhinged and consumed the entirety of Oxylem's face.

I wanted to stop him but my whole body was frozen to the spot, paralyzed by horror. Marcus's silence filled my ears.

Delano unlatched from Oxylem's body and tossed the dry husk into the waves. It was nothing more than a hunk of driftwood now. We both watched it bob out to sea. The seconds passed like hours. My mind had gone numb.

"Look at me," Delano said. "Quickly, before it's over."

Without thinking, I did as he asked. His long dark hair shimmered into golden laurels, the way Oxylem's must have been before he lost himself.

"Beautiful, isn't it?" Delano twined a lock around his finger and smiled fondly. "He was always a lovely boy, but he would never have survived. He was too sweet. Too gentle. Too unwilling to fight." His smile turned into a mirthless chuckle. "I forced him to grow up because I knew he couldn't. And after he inevitably failed, I would be able to take his essence as my own."

Something clicked in my head, and I gasped. "You're stealing their power," I said. "This is why you're killing the gods."

"Why else?" he asked as if it were the most obvious thing in the world. "Their only usefulness to me comes in the form of what I can take from them. I am a vessel, my darling. They are the waters of tribute." He gazed pensively at the ships. "It took you a long time to find these, you know. I was worried that perhaps you had lost some of the razor's edge that had brought you so far. I admit I underestimated you, for here you are after all—the only thing in this horrid world that has yet to disappoint me." He glanced at me and raised an eyebrow. "That said, if you wanted to know my grand plan so much, all you needed to do was ask." He laughed, the sound simultaneously menacing and musical.

"Spill it, then," I said crossly. The shock had slowly

worn off, and the remnants of my patience were danger-ously thin.

"They were for my army," he said simply. "Hyrrik's abundance of manpower combined with Oxylem's resources produced magnificent results." He beamed at the ships in the manner of a proud parent. "They are perfect. Exquisite. I planned to load them up and send them to the Asian coastline. Not a single god has managed to gain and keep a foothold on that whole continent. There is no oppo-sition. My following would have swelled by the millions. From there, on to the seat of the world."

"Yeah, screw that," I said. "I'll burn every last one of these ships."

Delano laughed again, utterly nonplussed. "Do as you please," he said serenely. "You're a fool if you think this is my only plan. Indeed, it is but one of many. And every day, my power grows. No mere human can dream of stopping me." His roving eyes settled on me and cut through to my core the way they had that first time at the slaughterhouse. "Darling Vic. I wonder what you'll taste like."

I suppressed a disgusted shudder. "The only thing you'll taste is this sword."

Delano smiled indulgently. "Yes. Soon enough."

I scowled. That wasn't the kind of response I'd hoped for. He didn't give me the chance to reply. The great wings on his back beat up a whirlwind, and in the next instant, he was gone, had risen out of sight into the murky sky.

"*Fuck* that guy," I said and rubbed my hands over my eyes. "Shit."

CHAPTER THIRTY-SEVEN

I sat down on the damp rock and didn't care that my ass was soaked in less than a minute. Dry asses were for winners, and I had let Delano escape.

The ocean lapped at the smooth edge of the shore and tugged at Oxylem's abandoned boat. Having nothing else to do, I retied the rope to the best of my ability. Someone in this community probably had some use for it. Maybe Smitty could use it to fish or something.

My head still reeled from Delano, from seeing what he had turned into and hearing the extent of his plans for the future. I had trouble wrapping my mind around the reality that he consumed other gods and condensed them into… what? I sure as hell didn't know, and neither did Marcus.

I have never seen anything like this, the centurion admitted. *And although I am not sure what we could do in opposition, I feel that we should remain here for a while to guard against his return. At least then, we could attempt to issue a warning.*

"Yeah," I said absently. I was simply grateful for the quiet and the solitude. It was the kind of tranquility I hadn't truly experienced since we'd arrived at Fort Victory. It felt amazing to lean back on my hands, close my eyes, and decompress to the sound of the sea. The salt breeze cleansed my tension, and I embraced it.

Besides, I knew it wouldn't be long before the others looked for me. The Weres followed their noses toward the briny scent of the water and found the shoreline first. The rest of our forces followed. Luis's trucks rolled across the rocks and pulled into a neat line facing Delano's abandoned fleet. I glanced over my shoulder to see him and Deacon get out of one of the vehicles.

"Hey, Vic." Luis gave me a one-armed hug. "Man, I'm glad to see you." He studied the ships, his brow furrowed. "What the hell is this crap? Are we going to be pirates?"

I smirked. "No, matey. This was meant to be an armada, but we took down the soldiers meant to fill those ships. And possibly, we saved all of Asia in the process."

"Aw, yeah." Luis high-fived me. "That's how we roll in this gang." He stopped short. "Uh, this club. We're a club."

Deacon burst out laughing. "Like hell, we're a damn club." He turned to me and slipped an arm around my waist. "Tell me what we're doing with these things. I'm sure you have some ideas."

I shrugged. "Not really. I figure we can take them apart and use all the lumber for something else. Houses, maybe. It'd free up some space in the church."

"I bet you could get some of those big tree-looking homies to help," Luis suggested. "The giant ones, you know? Like real-ass trees. We had a damn field day trying to pick them off, but many them surrendered after the fight anyway 'cause I guess they didn't want to die. I think that jackass brainwashed them."

"They *do* look like they could break down some ships, don't they?" I asked. "I'll run it by Smitty when I see him." I craned my neck over Deacon's shoulder and searched for the blacksmith's white head. He stood and took stock of the empty ships with Brax on one side and Amber on the other. She beamed with her whole face as usual. Nothing could keep that girl down for long, not even being kidnapped and almost killed by a god.

We drove back to the church in the trucks. During the ride, Deacon dressed the cut on my arm and I filled them in on the Delano front as much as I could. "Things don't look good for the rest of the world right now," I concluded. "We need to figure out a way to stop him, or else he will take over."

"I'm still stuck on the fact that you saw him eat a dude," Luis said.

I ran my good hand through my hair. "Me too, honestly. I didn't know gods could get even more powerful than they already were. We'll have to come up with some serious innovations."

"We'll do it," he said and flashed me a cheesy grin in the rearview mirror. "He can keep sticking parts on all he likes. He can't make himself invincible."

He may get close, Marcus said. *But the brave young man is correct. True invincibility has eluded the gods forever. Its achievement would be a feat far beyond Delano's current power.*

"That simply means he won't quit anytime soon," I said. "But neither will we. Wherever that shithead turns up, we'll be there too."

Luis gave a thumbs-up. "That's the spirit, chief. If there's one thing I've learned in my life, it's that no one runs forever."

The first thing I did when I got back was to go to the bell tower and try the radio. As I fiddled with the dial, a transmission from Namiko came through. "Anyone there at White Wolf Point?" she asked. "I have a message to relay from Fort Victory."

"Oh, hey," I said. "I was trying to get through."

"You sound tired, Vic. Maya wanted me to let you know that Frank and Steph got back to the fort earlier today."

"Nice!" I sat up straighter. "Did she say whether they found anything?"

"Apparently, there's news," Namiko replied. "I don't know what it is. According to Maya, it's too risky to transmit over the air."

I sighed and smiled. "Ahh, I should have known. Thanks, Namiko. It sounds like it's time for us to hit the road back home." I paused. "By the way, I like the name you picked for this place."

"It was either that or Smitty's Cove," she said. "Safe travels. Let me know when you're back east."

I went down the stairs with a full mind, so distracted that I almost bowled into a certain FBI agent coming up. "Just the woman I wanted to see," he said with a smile.

"Steph and Frank are back," I told him. "They have sensitive news. We have to get back to the fort ASAP."

"Is that what you look so worried about?" he asked as he smoothed a lock of my hair back. "We'll handle that when it comes. Right now, there's something else we need to discuss."

I raised my eyebrows. "There is?"

"Sure is." He started to back me up the steps again. "I have a rain check I'd like to cash."

I was laughing when he leaned over and pressed his lips to mine and pulled me close against his body. Without hesitation, I wrapped my arms around his neck and savored the sensation. We lingered in that intimate space after it was over, then he kissed me once more and murmured, "Gotta make up for lost time."

I nuzzled his neck tenderly. "You ready to head home, St. Clare?"

He held me a little tighter. "As long as you're there," he said, "I'll go anywhere."

Heat was practically a foreign entity on Joel's skin after so many days spent trekking through the blasted wilderness, but *damn*, it felt good. He'd lost track of how long it had been since he and Gina left civilization behind—a week, maybe? Ten days? It didn't really matter. They were tired, starved, and cold to the bone. To be inside an actual building felt like a religious experience.

"Holy shit," Gina whispered. "I can't believe we made it." She'd bundled up in a thick woolen blanket after they went through Intake, and the color returned to her lips. Slowly, she squeezed his hand.

"Yeah." He looked around at the room they walked through. "Why's it so empty in here, though? This place looked huge on the outside." In fact, the fortress' stern, militant façade had been incredibly intimidating to approach—under kinder circumstances, he might have urged Gina to keep moving. They'd been greeted by armed guards, to say nothing of the snipers in the tower at the gate. He had thought for sure that they would be shot.

But they were welcomed instead. On the inside, he smelled something that made his stomach gurgle painfully. Gina caught a whiff of it too. She tugged on his sleeve. "Let's go see if we can get some of whatever that is," she said. "I could literally eat anything right now." She followed the scent toward a hallway on the left.

"What if they're cooking all the new people?" he asked with a slight grin. It was a joke, mostly, but it would explain why there hadn't been a line a mile long to get into the place.

Gina poked him in the ribs. "Don't be morbid. Everyone we've met so far has been super nice."

"We've met like three guards. And they all had guns." Joel didn't want to be the guy who looked a gift fort in the mouth, but he'd seen enough slasher and doomsday films to be aware of the potential consequences.

Gina, for her part, was adamant. "I'd be more worried if they didn't," she told him. "Chill out, Joel. Don't get lost in your own head. We haven't died in the middle of nowhere, and that's good enough for me right now."

"Okay, okay." He shrugged and allowed her to lead him farther down the corridor. Light glowed from the crack beneath the double doors at the end. As they approached, one of the doors opened a crack, enough to allow a woman to slip out. She stopped when she saw the two newcomers. A big smile spread across her face. Her thick red hair was piled on top of her head.

"Welcome," she said and stepped forward to shake their hands. "The guys told me we had some new arrivals." She studied them quickly. "I'm Veronica. And you look as hungry as hell if I do say so myself."

"Yes," Gina said immediately.

The woman laughed. "Well, that's a problem we can fix. Come on in, but try to keep quiet. Vic's about to give a speech, I think."

"Vic?" Joel furrowed his brow. "I think I've heard that name before."

"Damn right you have," said the redhead, her hand on the door. "She's fought her ass off since the beginning. It's about time word started to get around."

Gina gasped. "She's the one who cleared New York! I heard she saved a ton of refugees."

"She sure did. So you want to meet them?" The woman pushed the door open to reveal the crowded mess hall beyond. It was full to the gills, and every eye was turned toward the front.

"Wait," said Joel. "Vic's a girl?" He promptly received an elbow in the ribs. "Hey, ouch! I didn't know."

Veronica shushed him. "Food line's up there," she said quietly and pointed. "But you'll want to hear this."

"Is that really her?" Gina's eyes were wide.

"In the flesh," Veronica confirmed. She ushered them in. "Go on. "

Joel kept walking, his gaze now riveted to the front of the room along with everyone else's. A woman stood there with a microphone in hand and looked at the crowd. She was almost tall, her green eyes framed by dark hair pulled back into a careless ponytail. The clothes she wore were clean, but she had bandages on her face and wrapped around her right arm. She seemed totally unfazed by the attention focused on her like a laser, probably because a working cell phone was an oddity at this point, let alone any kind of camera. Her speech would likely go unrecorded.

After she started talking, Joel thought that was a shame. He stopped filling his plate to watch her, and he noticed Gina did the same. The woman spoke with strong, fiery confidence, her eyes full of conviction. She turned every now and then to capture each onlooker with her captivating gaze.

"From this point on, there will be no more battles and no more skirmishes," she declared. "We are through scrapping in streets and alleys or building barricades to defend our homes. I have had the privilege to witness the strength of humanity firsthand, in New York and across the country. I've learned that people will rise if they are given an example. They will mold themselves in the image of those whom they admire, and they will fight like hell for ideals they believe in and rights they deserve." She paused and glanced at the rapt audience. "It's time for us to make that happen. Rise up. Fight like hell. Kill Delano and win the war."

The cheer that went up around Joel was thunderous. For days afterward, it echoed in his ears.

I'm ST Branton, silent partner on the Forgotten Gods series. Normally Chris and Lee keep me locked in the dungeon, hands tied to the typewriter (they ARE good friends, thanks for asking). But they let me out for special occasions.

And this is a special occasion.

While you've been reading Haunted by the Gods (how about that Vic Stratton, huh? Isn't she great? If only she'd come here and use that sword on these chains…), I've been hard at work on the epic conclusion to the Forgotten Gods saga.

And I'm almost finished.

That's right! Forgotten Gods Book 8 will soon be upon us, and I've gotta say, it's a doozie. It's got some sadness, plenty of sweetness, and a whole heck of a lot of action. I think you're going to like it.

So if you've got friends as good as my pals Chris and Lee, this might be a great chance to recommend Forgotten Gods to them. Or you could head on over to Amazon or

Good Reads and leave a review. And while you're at it, write to congress and ask them about investigating the plight of authors chained in basements (kidding Lee!).

For Kronin!
STB

<u>Steel City Heroes Saga</u>

The Catalyst
<u>Buy The Catalyst</u>

The Crucible
<u>Buy The Crucible</u>

The Casting
<u>Buy The Catalyst</u>

<u>Jack Carson Stories</u>

The Devil's Due
<u>Buy The Devil's Due</u>

The Devil's Wager
<u>Buy The Devil's Wager</u>

<u>The Rise of Magic</u>
*** With Michael Anderle ***

<u>Restriction (01)</u>
Reawakening (02)
Rebellion (03)

CONNECT WITH CM RAYMOND AND LE BARBANT

Email List:

www.subscribepage.com/smokeandsteelnews

Facebook:

Come hang out on the Forgotten Gods Facebook page:
www.facebook.com/ForgottenGodsSeries/

Website:

www.smokeandsteel.com